To the Dead City

The First Book of the Glyst Saga

Alex Bentley

For updates and free stories, visit: theglyst.com

Chapter One

Seven Cuts and Seven Cups

As we move deeper into the Freewood, I think of how I will never be like my father. Not because he is a man and I am a girl—even though I have received the Seven Cuts and filled the Seven Cups—but because he is fearless and I am afraid. I have been afraid every day for the last three of my sixteen years. But my father doesn't know this. Nobody knows. I hide my fear, burying it as a crow buries its food.

"Alys," my father whispers. "Look. There." With a massive hand, he points at the highest branches of an oak, a furlong from where we've been squatting patiently for the last hour. The tree is tall and strong but, like everything that grows in the Freewood, it has an air of sickness to it, as if something is amiss beneath the bark. The Tanwood, on the other side of the river, is lush and abundant, the trees that grow there sturdy, the animals caught there clad in sweet, tender flesh. The animals in the Freewood are tough, stringy and flavourless. Like the welpa up there in the sick oak tree, the one that my father is pointing at as if it's a miracle.

"I see it," I tell him, and nock an arrow.

He shakes his head, then smiles.

"Next time," he says.

I understand. We are in need of food, and my aim is not as true as his. I lower my bow but keep the arrow nocked.

My father slides an arrow from the quiver on his back. The quiver is made from the grey, matted skins of several welpa, stitched together with thick, woollen thread. He nocks the arrow and draws. The quiver is shoddy, but the bow is strong and fine. My father made it himself when he was my age. He aims. He waits. He waits. Waits. Then he releases the string.

The welpa throws back its head and opens its long, black muzzle to signal its distress or to warn its kin, but no sound emerges. Its spindly limbs wilt and it drops to the forest floor with a thud-rustle, autumn leaves rising in something like a circle around the dead creature, then settling again.

"Bag it," says my father, nocking another arrow.

The welpa is dead, my father knows this. But he also knows that the scavengers in the Freewood are swift and dangerous.

I slide the arrow back into my quiver and shoulder the bow. Running in a half-crouch and keeping wide of my father's line of sight, I race toward the lifeless welpa. I am not fearless like my father, but I am faster than him. I am faster than anyone in Gafol. The Jarl of Gafol says this is because I filled the Seven Cups and have less blood now, lightening my load, but I was the fastest long before the cuts. I used to think the Jarl was wise. Now I am certain he is a fool. A selfish, lazy fool. The Seven Cuts are symbolic, they don't actually *do* anything. Unless you count almost killing you as doing something.

I don't know if you have the Ritual of the Seven Cuts and the Seven Cups in your part of Abegan. It is a cruel and needless ceremony, one that I now think is not intended to transform but kill, to remove an embarrassing problem.

When a husband and wife have only one child, and that child is a girl, life is hard. For example, a girl cannot accompany her father when he hunts in the Freewood and bag his game. That is the duty of the son. If my father had to bag his own game, he wouldn't be able to keep watch for slite and nef and other things with teeth and claws, and he would be vulnerable. A hunter without a son in the Freewood will find his death. Even a hunter as proficient as my father. A man without a son cannot bequeath his sword and must fight in every conflict regardless of infirmity. When a man without a son dies, everything he owns becomes the property of the Jarl, even the man's wife. The prospect of this weighs heavily on the sonless man, and he dies prematurely, bringing to pass that which he dreaded all the sooner. It is a wretched thing to be a man without a son.

I could tell you in the most academic terms about the Ritual of the Seven Cuts and the Seven Cups. I could give you an entirely dispassionate account, but I feel that would miss the point. The point of the ceremony is pain and degradation.

They woke me early. The sun was little more than a nick on the horizon, bleeding a little light onto the fields in the distance, not quite reaching the thatched roofs of the roundhouses of Gafol. They took me, naked, to the Jarl's hall and strung me up like a hog or a foorstig, feet to the rafters, crown to the earth. And the Jarl cut me seven times with a whetted flint so thin it was almost invisible, and those spectators at the back of the hall might have thought he inflicted those gushing wounds with a stroke of his fingertips. The first cut was from my hairline to the nape of my neck. The noise it made, the passage of that razored flint, was not unlike the sound of a fish being gutted. But it was louder. I could hear that sound in the centre of my skull, the middle of my mind, and, ever since, in my dreams and nightmares. The second cut was to my left wrist, a bloody torc. The third was to the right wrist. The fourth ran down the soft flesh of the inner portion of my upper left arm, ending at the elbow, beginning at the armpit. The fifth reflected the fourth on my right arm. The sixth was deep and long across my belly, as you might have seen on a mother whose child was stubborn at birth. The final cut, the seventh cut, was really two cuts, a seventh and an eighth, but delivered as a single slash across the middle of my thighs. It bothers me, more than it should, that the Ritual of the Seven Cuts and the Seven Cups comprises eight cuts. It makes a lie of the whole thing.

Blood ran into my mouth, up my nose, into my eyes. I had to keep spitting and snorting to stop myself from being suffocated. But a part of me was glad of the blood, because it hid my tears. I did not want the Jarl or the people of Gafol to see my tears; nor my mother and father.

Seven clay cups were placed beneath me, or so my father told me. I was oblivious by that point. I was cold and hot, terrified and sleepy. I was this, and I was that, all at once. I was aware of applause and hoots. These were the sounds I'd once heard when my mother had told me to accompany my father to the Festival of Seros to make sure he came home unscathed, the sounds the men had made as he'd gulped far too much mead from the horn of a goat.

Only when the cups were full did the applause and the hooting cease, and only then were my wounds cleaned and bound. I drifted in and out of sleep for I don't know how many days. I remember the Jarl chanting the Verses of Wealm somewhere high above me, a look on his face that fell somewhere between apology and certainty. Alys is dead, that face cried out. How awful. How expected.

But I wasn't dead. My father wouldn't have to go to war when he was old and infirm. His belongings and his wife would not become the property of the Jarl. And he would have someone to accompany him when he hunted in the Freewood.

I grab the welpa and push it into the strong, woollen bag my mother made last year. My mother will never be the property of the Jarl. She died three months ago, and that was that. I remember how she screamed when they dragged me to the Ritual. Dragged me, though I'd volunteered. The dragging was part of it, I suppose. She never cried. She shrieked, and she ranted, but she did not sob. She cried a little on the day she died, as the thing deep inside her, the thing that smelled terrible and she told us was made of hot spikes, shifted and grew and stopped her from breathing. The only time I ever saw her cry with abandon was when I won the Five Eagle Feathers as the fastest runner in Gafol when I was just nine years old and still my father's daughter.

"Alys!"

I am pulling the drawstring tight on the bag I watched my mother make when my father cries out. I don't have to see the slite to know it's there. The smell is more than sufficient. The smell—like rotted mushrooms and deep earth—and the sound in my father's voice that I refuse to believe is fear. Alarm, yes, but not fear.

The slite rears up on its hind legs so it stands taller than our roundhouse. I glimpse its fishbelly-white flesh through the shaggy blankets of moss and fern that have grown on its pale hide over what must be decades. It's an old one, and the old ones are clever. It could have snagged the welpa and run, could have stolen our supper. But it waited. For a bigger meal. Its antlers look like deadwood— and that's just what I'd thought I'd seen as I approached the welpa: a pile of moss-carpeted deadwood—but they are not brittle as deadwood. A slite's antlers are hard as rock, and sharp. They sharpen them against the Wyrsan Stones that stand at the heart of the Freewood, the stones that some say are the reason for the forest's sickness and some say are just stones.

It drops back down onto four legs and charges. In the same instant, an arrow thuds into its rump. My father shouts something, but I don't hear it over the thunderous snort of the slite. I don't hear it, but I know what his instruction would be. Leave the welpa. I do just that, and dart left, going instinctively to where the forest is thicker, where there is less room for the slite to manoeuvre, increasing my chances of survival. Leaving the welpa behind has also made it marginally less likely that I'll die. If I can outrun the thing for long enough, it will be forced to decide: continue to pursue me and potentially eat nothing or return to the place of ambush and a guaranteed meal. Not as tasty and satisfying a meal as me, but better than an empty stomach.

If I had not bled into the Seven Cups and lived, my father would be alone now, and he can't run as fast as me. Nobody can run as fast as me. I have the Five Eagle Feathers hanging above my bed to prove it.

And even as I speed into the forest, I realise my mistake.

The slite isn't following me. If it were following me, I would feel the droplet-heavy clouds of its foetid breath against the back of my neck. I would hear its snorts and the gnashing of its long, black teeth. I risk a glance over my shoulder.

The slite is charging toward my father.

My father, knowing he cannot outrun it, looses two arrows before the thing is upon him. Both find their target, but the slite is unimpressed. It twists its head and swipes with its antlers.

My father throws his bow left and lurches right, hoping the twin movements might confuse the beast. It doesn't. As I thought, old and therefore clever. The slite's antlers, sharpened on the Wyrsan Stones, catch my father's shoulder, but only just, and the strap of his quiver takes the brunt of the damage. The quiver falls, scattering arrows. My father is moving fast now, circling round the beast and drawing his sword. He hacks twice at the slite's mossy hide before it turns to face him once more. It lashes out with its antlers once more, but he skips back and they miss him by inches.

I am only a few yards from my father, drawing my knife, when the slite slashes with its antlers and lunges forward in a single undulating motion. I see its eyes, huge, yellow and mad. I see steam and snot erupt from its flaring nostrils. I see its antlers—how could I ever have mistaken them for deadwood?—slash at my father's chest.

He spins, facing me now and, for the first time in my life, I see fear in his eyes. His tunic is ragged where the antlers gouged it and glistening red with blood. The sword that had once been his father's hangs limp in his hand, but he does not drop it.

"Run!" he yells.

Chapter 2

The Stone Has Hit the Lake

I do as my father tells me. I run. But not in the direction he intended.

I run toward him.

The slite rises up on its hind legs, looming over my father like the waves at Brim, the moment before they crash against the cliffs with that tremendous noise that my mother told me was the voice of a drowned god, its name long forgotten, its misery eternal.

My father turns back to face the beast, lifting his sword. He finds a gap in the slite's shaggy hide, a glimpse of pale flesh, and rams his sword into its belly. The blade disappears to the hilt. A foul green-black liquid gushes from the wound, and the slite lets out a thick, wet shriek. My father tries to retrieve his sword, but the grip is slick, and he staggers back weaponless.

The slite, snorting blood now, drops onto all fours and slams its granite skull into my father's already mutilated chest. My father is lifted from the ground and sent several yards through the air, landing at my feet. His eyes are closed. His mouth, filled with blood, hangs open.

The slite stalks toward him, toward me, but already its legs are failing, its snorts becoming frequent and shallow. It lists left and crashes onto its side. My father's sword is expelled from its belly in a fountain of that green-black liquid. The smell is atrocious, as when an animal geds itself at slaughter, and I am ashamed to find it reminds me of my mother's breath in the days approaching her death.

I want to go to my father, but I can't take my eyes off the slite, suddenly certain it will lurch back to its feet and charge at me with its not-deadwood antlers. I run to my father, my knife in my hand, and now that I have reached him, I can do nothing because I am afraid.

Blood spurts from the slite's nostrils and I am reminded of the Ritual, of the blood running into my nose. The wound in the slite's gut gapes, and I am reminded of the Ritual, of the cut across my own belly. The slite's mad, yellow eyes roll back into its long skull, and I am reminded of the Ritual, of the Seventh Cup filled and my consciousness draining from me, as if my very self had been housed in my veins all along and not in my head as I had always thought.

I look at the slite and I am reminded of the Ritual.

But, if I'm being honest, when I look at *anything* I am reminded of the Ritual. I am always thinking of the Ritual.

The Ritual of the Seven Cuts and the Seven Cups.

That cruel and pointless endeavour.

Why couldn't they have just let me hunt with my father as I was? Why couldn't they have just let me fight in my father's place *as I was*? Why did they have to fill my sleep with nightmares? Why did they have to make me afraid? I was of more use to my father *before* the Ritual. The process that had made me worthy in the eyes of the Jarl, those eyes through which all his ancestors stared, had made me worthless in my own eyes and useless in reality. Before the Ritual, I was so free of fear, I *volunteered* to be cut and bled. After, I jumped at shadows and the sight and smell of blood turned my stomach.

I am suddenly furious. And in my fury, I am unafraid.

I turn my back on the slite. If it rises, it rises. If it charges, it charges. If I die, I die.

I kneel at my father's side. He is still alive. His chest is rising and falling but, like the slite, his breathing is shallow. His eyes are closed, but there is a flickering behind his eyelids.

One of his arms has fallen across his chest. I lift it so I might better see the wound. I wish I hadn't. There is bone visible in the mess of blood and muscle. This is a deathwound. On the field of battle, a fallen warrior's companion would touch the tip of their sword to the wound and say, "Wealm is here. His cold hand touches me. But not as it has touched this man. Blessed be Wealm." But I say nothing. I don't feel the cold touch of Wealm. I still feel the fury, and it is as hot as a new-forged blade in the moments before it is quenched. I feel that heat in my chest, in my heart. Then it begins to spread. Down into my gut, up into my skull. It ripples down my arms to my fingertips and, without thinking about it, an act of pure intuition, I sink my suddenly burning fingers into my father's wound.

There is a hiss.

Steam rises from the wound.

My father's legs begin to twitch.

Behind his eyelids, his eyes move with the frantic energy of trapped insects.

And then I am no longer in the Freewood. I am no longer with my father.

I am nowhere.

A vast expanse of blackness stretches out in all directions. I look down at myself and there is no 'myself' to see. I try to hold out my hands in front of my eyes. There are no hands to hold out, no eyes with which to see them. There is nothing, just nothing, and I am part of it. I have fainted, I decide. Or I have gone mad. Or I have gone mad and fainted. Or died and gone to such a place as the mad go when they pass. Perhaps I am deep underwater with the drowned god at Brim. Does it matter? And, anyway, it isn't so bad. I feel calm. For the first time since the Ritual, I feel calm. I feel like I used to feel in those sweet moments just before I'd drift off to sleep, when I could hear my mother and father talking, and sometimes laughing, as they carried on about their various tasks after I'd been put to bed. It is like a folding-in of the self into a secret, warm place of safety and troublelessness. I would smile if I had a mouth with which to smile and sigh if I had lungs with which to sigh. Is this what it would have been like if I'd succumbed to the Ritual of the Seven Cuts and the Seven Cups? Are these the Fields of Wealm? But I have not died in battle—unless the slite crept up on me and ended my life—and, anyway, where are the Great Orchards? Where are the Unrim, those bees the size of horses that the dead ride to the River of Honey? Where is my mother?

No, these are not the Fields of Wealm. This is nothing. This is Nowhere.

And that's fine. I am happy to be Nowhere.

I lose track of time. Perhaps there *is* no time here in the Nowhere. What purpose could time have in relation to nothing? Things happen from one moment to the next. When nothing is happening, what use are moments, what even is 'next'?

I lose track of time and time loses all meaning.

And then the Nowhere ripples.

There is an old turn of phrase that my father would use when discussing the marital strife of another couple: *the stone has hit the lake*. I remember when we could hear Bloma and Wessim Cropp shouting at each other from four roundhouses away, my father said to my mother, with rather too much satisfaction, "I told you, Alva. I told you, did I not? They were not a fit match, those two. The stone has hit the lake. Sooner than I thought, too." When I asked my mother about the phrase, she said, "It is one of the old turns, little Alys. It is about the Big Things. The Gods. Your father uses it in a silly way. Because he is a silly man. Sweet and silly."

The Nowhere ripples.

The stone has hit the lake.

It is about the Big Things. The Gods.

Suddenly, I am somewhere.

The transition is so abrupt I cry out like someone waking from the worst of nightmares.

I am somewhere. I am in the Freewood, upon my knees next to my dying father. Behind me, I can hear the slite's shallow, sticky gasps.

What happens next—now that there *is* a next, now that there *are* moments in which things *can* happen—surprises me, even though I am the one making it happen.

I lift my right hand, gloved in blood, from my father's wound and direct it to the slite, pointing at the creature with a dripping finger. My left hand, I flatten, splaying my fingers wide. And then I stop breathing. I do not 'hold my breath', I just stop taking breaths. My lungs are as still as a lake before it is struck by a stone.

Behind me, a voice, rumbling and wheezing, says, "It is coming."

My heart strikes my sternum hard, trying to break free of my chest. I turn.

There is no one there. Only the dying slite.

"It is coming."

The slite. The slite is speaking. It has no lips with which to shape the words, but it speaks them nonetheless.

"It is coming."

The blood in its mouth bubbles with each syllable, as if the words are emerging from its lungs, as if the words are its dying breaths.

"The Gravene," it says.

Then a ball of pale pink light, the size of an apple, lifts from the centre of the slite's forehead, as I have heard of swamp lights emerging from the black waters at Fenfellic that some say are the ghosts of those who wish they were dead but lack the courage to end their lives. The slite's body slumps into itself, as if all its offal and gizzards have withered to nothing, and the ball of light glides toward me. It stops an inch or two from my fingertips, hovering. It smells of blackberries and rose petals.

I stretch out toward it. Touch it.

And then I am looking up at the canopy of trees, the pale blue sky beyond. It is an afternoon sky, and we began our hunt in the small hours of the morning. I see a cloud shaped like a heart and I recall my mother telling me that seeing a heart-shaped cloud means love is looking for you from somewhere afar.

My father's face appears.

The blood on his chin and around his mouth and nose is dry. There is panic in his eyes.

"Alys!" he whispers harshly. "We have to go. The grefa stones will be whistling, and the Jarl will be looking for the reason why. We have to go, Alys. Now!"

Chapter 3

Of Maddy Things and Crawlies

I remember the first time I heard the whistling of the grefa stones.

I was six and helping my mother plant carrots at the back of our roundhouse, in the small patch of good ground which gets the sun and is sheltered from the wind. My mother was singing 'The Carrot Song' which she told me must be sung while planting carrots. I later found out she had invented the song on the spot because she could see I was getting bored with drilling holes and pushing down seeds.

> *We push the seed into the ground*
> *Into a hole an inch around*
> *Not too deep, not too deep*
> *We do not want the seed to sleep*
> *We want the seed to turn to shoots*
> *And reach down deeply with its roots*
> *We want the seed to become a carrot*
> *Carrot! Carrot! Carrot! Carrot!*

Six-year-old me found that last line hilarious, but now I suspect it came about because my mother couldn't think of a word that rhymed well with 'carrot'.

Then, in mid-verse, my mother stopped singing and straightened from her work, wincing a little at the pain in her back.

"What is it, Mammy?" I asked.

"Do you hear that?"

"What?"

"A whistling."

Her expression shifted by degrees from curiosity to alarm.

When next she spoke, her voice was quiet and flat. It wasn't exactly a whisper. It was more like she did not want to give the words weight. It was as if, perhaps, she was giving herself leave to deny she'd said them at all.

"The grefa stones," she said. Then, "Stay here, Alys. Carry on with the planting. Sing the Carrot Song."

She handed me the seeds and hurried away.

I could hear it myself then, the whistling, high and thin.

I made a big hole in the soil with my fist and dropped all the remaining seeds into it.

"There," I said, clapping the dirt from my palms, and followed my mother.

She was standing at the edge of the crowd that had formed outside the Jarl's squarehouse. To one side of my mother was Roisa. Roisa had been my best friend since we were babies, but the week before we had fought over a brooch we'd found in the brambles on the edge of the Freewood and had not spoken since.

"What's happening?" I asked her.

She glared at me.

"That was *my* brooch," she said. "I saw it first."

"You did *not*. *I* saw it first. What's happening?"

"The bowl full of grefa stones in the Jarl's squarehouse started whistling, and now he says we have to find the Maradyn before the Cwalee come."

Maradyn. Cwalee. I had heard these words before, but my mother and father had never schooled me in them, never knee-sat me and explained them as they did with all the other words and things in which I expressed a curiosity. I wondered why they had never done so, then realised I had never asked. And then I wondered why I had never asked.

I manoeuvred my way to the front of the crowd. The whistling was almost maddening now.

The Jarl was standing in the wide doorway of his home, a large wooden bowl held out in front of him, the bowl from which that strident whistling was coming. There was a painting of an eye on the side of the bowl, the pupil of which was a red triangle. The Jarl was strong then and mostly dark of beard, and his voice had yet to creak and wheeze. The last ten years have not favoured him.

"Men!" he commanded. "Each take a stone."

The men did as instructed. Including my father.

"You know what must be done," said the Jarl, once every man had his grefa stone. "Fetch your sword. Find the Glystgedder. And when you do, do not waver, do not shrink. Do that which must be done. For the good of Gafol and all the lands beyond. Go!"

The men dispersed, and the whistling of the grefa stones dispersed with them, like blood in water.

I felt a hand seize mine and looked up into my mother's face.

"Didn't I tell you to carry on with the planting?" she said.

"I did. All the carrots are planted."

"Let's go home," she said. "I do not want you to see what comes next."

"Why, Mammy? What comes next?"

"It doesn't matter. You are too little to hear of it."

"But Roisa knows," I complained. "And she is eight days younger than me. It's not fair. She knows all about the… Maddy Things? And the… Crawlies?"

"The Maradyns. And the Cwalee. It is not something you need to know about. When you are older, Alys."

I continued to harangue my mother for the rest of the journey home. I was very good at haranguing. Haranguing and running and wrestling brooches from the grip of my best friend's hand.

It was dark, and the stew my mother had made had gone cold in my father's bowl. I had only ceased my haranguing in order to eat and to listen to the distant whistles of the grefa stones.

My mother glared at me and sighed.

"Very well," she said. "If only to take my mind from what's being done… what's happening out there." She sat down in her chair by the hearth and gestured for me to sit in the chair opposite, my father's chair. I had never sat on it before without my father. It felt strange, too big. My legs dangled inches from the ground, and the heat from the fire warmed the soles of my feet.

"Once upon a time," I said.

"No," my mother said a little too quickly. "This is not a 'once upon a time' story. It matters when this thing happened. Because it was not in the dim past where the candle flame cannot reach. It was in the bright past, where candle flames are not needed because the sun still shines there. There are yet those alive who remember those days. They are very old those people and there are very few of them, but they are around."

"Old like Nanny Torr?" I asked.

"Older, but not by much. And there are none in Gafol. Not since Agnis Bron passed, and that was before you were born, when I was wee like you."

"Tell it," I said. Even at six, I knew my mother was stalling.

"Less than one hundred years ago, there used to be magic across the land, and people called it the Glyst. There were healers and seers. There were those who could make fire in the palm of their hand, and those that could talk to the beasts. There were those that could fly and those that could walk through walls. It was, according to all the stories, a wondrous time, when the Great Cities were built and the Big Roads were carved through the forests and hillsides, as a ploughshare cuts through the soft soil of a generous field. This time in our history is known as the Abundance because there was an abundance of Glyst and an abundance of all things *because* of the Glyst. Every town and village had its Glyster, sometimes more than one. A village Glyster might be able to heal a sick cow or encourage a crop to grow or hold back a frost. Glysting was a currency between villages. The Glyster of one village might mend the broken limb of another village's Jarl, and in return their Glyster would see that the harvest was good in the other village.

"The most proficient users of the Glyst — the Maradyns, as they were known — gathered in the Great Cities. There were schools there, clusters of huge spiralling towers, where Glysters could be taught to control their talent, improve it, and become Maradyns.

"The cities were where the Cwalee first appeared, stepping out from holes torn in the very air. It is said they were tall and thin and white, with too many joints in their limbs. Their heads were long and fleshless, and where a mouth should be were tentacles, as of the squid that can be netted at Brim. These tentacles could grow to any length it seemed, and with them they drained the Glyst from the Maradyns, drained the Glyst and the life. Those without the Glyst who stood in their way were dispatched as easily as you or I might dispatch an insect. And soon there were no Maradyns left, and the Great Cities were as tombs.

"And then the Cwalee came for the Glysters, in the towns and the villages. And soon there were no Glysters and no Glyst. The time that followed is called the Want, because it was a time of paucity and lack, a difficult time, though there are some that called it the Calend, which means 'opportunity' or 'beginning' in the old tongue.

"But we're lucky, little Alys, because we are living on the other side of those times. Life can be hard, but life is good. We work and receive the benefit of our labour. Thanks to the kindly nature of the Jarl."

It was years later that I understood that these last two sentences were uttered with the nettle sting of sarcasm.

"But," I asked, "what has all this to do with the grefa stones?"

"The stones whistle when the Glyst is near. And they whistle especially loudly when the Glyst is born."

"When a baby Glyst comes into the world?"

My mother smiled. "No. When the Glyst is born into a person. Like an idea might be born in your head."

I gave her my best confused look.

"Remember that time you decided to write 'stinky' on the back of our pig with the green dye I'd made for your father's cloak?"

I smiled.

"And," she continued, "when I asked you why you did it, you said…"

"I said, 'I don't know. It just came into my head'."

"Well, it is like that with the Glyst. It just comes into a person."

"And where have the men gone with the stones? What is Daddy doing?"

A darkness passed over my mother's face, like the shadow of a black cloud as it flies above the fields.

"I shall tell you when we've had some tea," she said, forcing a smile.

She must have made the tea with mamera leaves, which she normally used for herself when her back was particularly bothersome, because I fell asleep before I'd even finished the brew.

There was a little light creeping into our roundhouse when I was woken by my father lifting me from his chair. He smelled funny. It was a familiar smell but, in my groggy state, I couldn't place it. It wasn't the worst smell, but neither was it pleasant.

"Are you awake, little one?" he said. He sounded tired, and there was something in his voice that I didn't recognise. Unlike the smell, it wasn't something I knew but couldn't bring to mind. It was a new thing. "Are you awake, Alys?"

I pretended I was not.

"Is it done?" my mother asked.

"The whistling has stopped, has it not?"

"Is it done?" my mother asked again, clearly in no mood for questions in response to questions.

"Yes."

"Who?"

"Noola." My father spoke the name as if he were pulling it from his flesh, like a thorn.

"Noola Fynn?"

"Yes." Again, a thorn being pulled.

"That poor thing. And Dansk Fynn, did he stand in the way?"

"Of course."

"And?"

"He fought to the end."

"With who?"

"Me." Another thorn plucked.

There was a long silence between my mother and father. I almost drifted back to sleep in its span.

"And who…?"

"Noola?"

"Yes."

"Not I. I could not."

Another silence, then my mother said, "Thank the gods. Thank them all."

The next time I heard such relief in my mother's voice, it was after the Ritual of the Seven Cuts and the Seven Cups, when the Jarl said, with a thread of incredulity in his own voice, "She lives. Alys lives."

My father carried me to my bed, sliding me under the thick blankets.

Before I fell back to sleep, I recognised the smell. I'd smelled it a few months ago, when we'd slaughtered Stinky the Pig. It was the smell of blood.

Chapter 4

In the Freewood, Alone

"Alys!"

My father pulls at my arm, lifting me as easily as he lifted me from his chair all those years ago. He smells of blood now, too. His own. But the wound to his chest is now just a wound to his tunic. I remember my mother making that tunic and, for one silly moment, I worry she will be vexed at the state of it.

He sets me down on my feet and, when he is confident I will not collapse, he takes his scabbard, complete with sword, from his belt and fastens it to my belt, next to my dagger. To the other side of my belt, he ties his small need-bag, the one that contains his flints for making fire, medicinal herbs and such. He puts his waterskin over my shoulder, then takes my bow and casts it aside, replacing it with his own, and filling my quiver with his arrows.

I don't understand what's happening.

"Go south," he says. "If you can see the moss high on the trees as you run toward them—and you *must* run—you will be heading south."

I want to tell him I'm not stupid and know how to navigate the woods, but my mouth is dry and my tongue is asleep.

"In an hour or so, you should reach the River Woever," he continues. "Follow it east until you come to an abandoned bridge. Cross the river there. Be careful. The bridge, like the road it serves, has not been used since the Abundance, and its wood will be soft or brittle or both. The road will take you south-east. A few hours along, you'll see a roundhouse. It is set back and overgrown, so you will have to have your wits about you. That is where your Aunty Elsam lives. She has not seen you since you were six, but she will know you. She is not in the jurisdiction of any Jarl and fends for herself. You will be out of the reach of the grefa stones, and your aunty does not believe the Glyst is a threat. She will feed you and care for you. She is a horrible woman, make no mistake, but she is good and loves deeply."

My tongue finally stirs from its idleness.

"I don't understand any of this," I say and am embarrassed by how childlike I sound, how hopeless and afraid.

"You do," my father says. "You understand it all."

I nod.

I do understand. I have the Glyst. The grefa stones are whistling. And the men of Gafol are coming to slay me.

I understand. I just don't want it to be so.

"From where you will meet the river to the bridge is a long trek," says my father. "It will be nightfall before you reach the bridge. Do *not* travel by night. Find somewhere to hide and rest until dawn. Do *not* light a fire. A fire will attract interest."

He takes off his cloak and rolls it up.

"This will make a good-enough blanket," he says, and hands me the cloak.

It is his green cloak. The one that my mother made and coloured with the same dye with which I wrote 'stinky' on our pig. Without thinking, I slide the cloak between the small of my back and my quiver.

Then a thought occurs. A horrible thought that sends a frost down my spine and pulls my skin tight.

"What about the Crawlies?" I ask.

My father looks confused, and I realise my mistake.

"The Cwalee," I say. "They will come for me."

"They will not," my father replies. He sounds *almost* certain.

"They will not?"

"I do not *think* they will come. Your aunty is horrible and loving, and she is also honest. Speak to her about it."

"The Cwalee will not come for me?"

"No." And then again, resolutely, "No."

"Why? And how do you know? How does Aunty know?"

"There isn't time for this, Alys."

The need to know is as strong as when my mother wouldn't tell me about the Maddy Things and the Crawlies, stronger in fact. But unlike the irritation on my mother's face, the fear on my father's compels me to let the matter go. It will have to wait until tomorrow and I am with Aunty Elsam. But then another thought occurs. This one does not send frost down my spine but puts an ache in my stomach, like when I ate the cakes that had not cooled yet despite my mother's warning that my belly would not approve.

"What will you do?" I ask.

"Don't worry about that."

"Don't worry? But they will know. If I am gone, and the stones are no longer whistling, they will know. And they will know you helped me, and they will kill you."

"I'll tell them we saw someone in the Freewood, a man. A man making fire with his bare hands. A man with the Glyst. I'll say we chased him and he escaped, but after that I could not find you. I will make a pretence of searching for you for the rest of my life. And they will believe me, because my face will be a mask of sorrow until I die."

He grabs me then, my father, and pulls me to his chest. He emits a single sob, so quiet. And it is by far the worst sound I have ever heard in my sixteen years. Even worse than the sound of the razored flint being drawn across my scalp.

And then I hear, faint and in the distance, the whistling of grefa stones.

My father releases me and wipes tears from his eyes with the heels of his palms. He kisses my forehead hard, as if he wants to leave an impression there that will last long enough to see me to safety.

He hands me the sack with the bagged welpa.

"It will keep until you get to Aunty Elsam, and she will cook it up fine."

"What are you going to eat?" I ask, but I know that is the least of his problems.

"Go," he says, his voice soft and kind. "And may Eascus, God of these and all woods, be with you."

I go. I don't look back. I don't think I could bear to watch my father, cloakless and unarmed, fading away from me into the woods. But also, there's a part of me that thinks somehow everything is going to be all right. There has been some kind of mistake. I don't have the Glyst. I will not be hunted by the men of Gafol and put to the sword. All of this is going to be resolved. It *must*. That naivety propels me forward for a little over half an hour then collapses. Because I remember when I was strung upside down in the Jarl's squarehouse, thinking he isn't *really* going to cut me with that flint. I remember thinking everything was going to be all right. I remember thinking there had been some kind of mistake.

This is real. This is happening. I am alone in the Freewood, and I am being hunted.

And what if my father is wrong about the Cwalee? What if they do come for me? What if they are coming for me right now from wherever it is they dwell? I imagine it just as my mother had described: the very air tearing open in front of me and one of those things—tall and thin and white, with too many joints in its limbs, head long and fleshless, and tentacles where a mouth should be—stepping out onto the decaying carpet of the forest floor and *reaching* for me. My mother had never described the creature's fingers, but my imagination, generous and cruel, provides the details. The fingers are, like its limbs, too long and with too many joints. It has two thumbs, one on either side of the hand, and in place of fingernails it has thin, black barbs, like the stinger of a straggis wasp.

For a few minutes, I cannot move. Fear has made me rigid as old, badly maintained leather. Then the whistling of the grefa stones starts up again, closer now. I run, and I do not stop until I can no longer hear that infernal whistling. I do not stop until I hear the River Woever. It is a loud river, fast-moving over many rocks.

I make my way down to the banks of the river and, kneeling in the mud and stones, splash water on my face. Then I head east. I will keep moving until nightfall. I will follow every one of my father's instructions and I will be with my Aunty Elsam in the morning. And everything will be fine.

Provided my father is not wrong, and the Cwalee are not coming.

They must be hungry, wherever they are. They ate over a hundred years ago and have not eaten since.

I shake my head. Such thoughts are unhelpful, I tell myself. Put your trust in your father, you little brat. I feel a surge of anger at myself, and that's good. The anger keeps the fear at bay.

I make good progress, and for the hour or so I have been following the river, I have not once heard the whistling of the stones. I almost begin to feel something like confidence. And then I realise I would not be able to hear the whistling of the stones, not this close to the rushing water.

The men of Gafol could be converging on me even now, swords and axes in hand. An arrow might be in flight at this very moment, and I would not know until it struck.

I look up into the woods and see movement everywhere. But it is high in the trees where a mild wind is toying with the leaves and tugging at the weaker branches. I scour the forest, as I would when hunting, looking for telling details and refusing to see the whole. *When hunting*, my father once said, *the whole is distracting. You must see it one piece at a time. Your game is never in 'the forest'; it is in a tree or a bush or behind a rock.*

And so I look from tree to tree, bush to bush, rock to rock, and I force my hearing to filter out the sounds of the Woever behind me.

There are no men, and I cannot hear the grefa stones.

"Lucky," I say. "Lucky, Alys. And luck is a bucket with a hole."

I resolve to follow the river from a distance from this point forward, keeping it just in view, just in earshot.

It is only because I decide it would be sensible to fill my waterskin before leaving the river behind that I turn and see the scabwolf rising from the water.

Chapter 5

Depending on Lady Blackbelly

It would be a pitiable thing, the scabwolf, if it were not for its considerable size, twice that of a man.

It is almost entirely hairless, and its pale pink hide is patched with weeping sores. Its eyes are yellow and rheumy, set deep in sockets that speak of unimaginable hunger. But the things that make it pitiable are what make it dangerous. Scabwolves are born with a worm in the belly which eats most of what the wolf eats, a greedy, uninvited guest. That worm, sometimes called a flaythread, geds out a poison, which the scabwolf is able to tolerate, if only just. The flaythread's venom finds its way into the scabwolf's slobber. And so a bite from a scabwolf is a very terrible thing.

Every instinct tells me to turn and run.

But the teachings of my father command me otherwise.

If I turn and run, the thing will be upon me in no time. Its eyesight is poor. Likewise, its sense of smell. But its hearing is keen. As if to demonstrate this, the scabwolf tips its head first left, then right. Listening. Then it bares its brown-yellow teeth.

They are long enough to pierce my arm and see their way through to the other side.

Suddenly it seems eminently sensible to ignore the teachings of my father. Running seems not only to be a viable option, but the only thing that can be done. As if my body has already decided the outcome of any debate, the muscles in my calves tense and my torso begins to turn.

But the riverbank is steep and muddy.

I might be the fastest runner in Gafol and have the Five Feathers to show for it, but I will not outrun a scabwolf on such a gradient with mud and water beneath my feet.

And still my calves tense and my body turns.

I glance back at the scabwolf. It stares at me with eyes that would not know the difference between a man and a tree stump, but it does a very good pretence of seeing. It snorts the air. Another pretence. It is a lie, this thing. Even its hunger belongs to the flaythread in its belly. And, for a moment, I am reminded of the Jarl. I don't know why. Regardless, it is enough to lend me sufficient anger that my calves relax a little and I turn to face the beast.

It tips its head left, then right again.

I wonder if it can hear my heartbeat, which sounds to me like the beating of huge hands on a kanna drum.

Abruptly, its head snaps to its right, looking eastward along the Woever. Or *listening* eastward. I see a fish, a Lady Blackbelly, drop back into the water, doubtless having leapt to snatch midges from the air. The scabwolf does not move in the fish's direction; it does not move at all, but its attention is not on me for the moment.

Holding my breath, I unshoulder my bow. Not *my* bow. My father's bow. It is heavier than mine, and unfamiliar. The grip is thick and makes my hand feel small, like a child's.

The scabwolf continues to glare eastward.

I reach back and pinch an arrow between thumb and forefinger.

I hear the scrape of the arrowhead against the neighbouring shaft. It is a tiny noise, a thin noise. But the scabwolf's head snaps in my direction as surely as it had at the splash of the Lady Blackbelly.

I freeze.

The scabwolf pretends to stare at me. It is an excellent pretence. Almost completely convincing. My heart is beating so hard now I can feel it in my belly and in the tips of the fingers that are squeezing the nock of the arrow. I want so badly to swallow, but I dare not. The click in my throat would be as sharp and as loud as a click of the fingers.

I wait. I wait for a noise, for anything to distract the beast.

But the Lady Blackbelly has gone down to the riverbed now to eat her mouthful of midges and will not be leaping again soon.

The scabwolf pretends to sniff the air.

As if it has caught my scent, it takes one step forward. Then another.

My throat is so dry with the need to swallow it itches. My eyes water.

The scabwolf tips its head left, then right. One ragged ear twitches like the leg of a dying thing, and I wonder what it has detected, and know it can only be my heartbeat or the tiny trickling sound of the single tear that is making its way down my cheek.

It takes another step forward.

I can smell it now.

It is the stink of an untreated wound. My stomach clenches at the foul odour.

I wish I'd run earlier, when the thing first emerged from the Woever. I might have made it up the riverbank and away. It's possible, with a little luck and no slipping.

But luck is a bucket with a hole and not to be relied upon.

An expression of my mother's pops into my head.

We are nowhere other than here.

She would use it whenever there was some problem which could only be tackled head on and could not be shirked. Like when I'd stood on a nail and there was nothing to do but pull it from my foot in one good, swift tug, no matter how much I told her I could get used to it or that it might just come out on its own while I slept.

We are nowhere other than here.

So I wait. With nothing to do and nowhere else I can possibly be.

The scabwolf takes another step forward.

A few more steps and I will be able to reach out and touch the tip of its dripping snout.

My shoulder stiffens and the muscles in my upper arm begin to burn. I start to feel dizzy and realise I have not taken a breath since I first caught the scabwolf's putrid tang. I let my lips open a little, just a slit, and take in a few threads of air. Just enough to keep me conscious, not enough to set my guts roiling.

I wonder why the scabwolf hasn't leapt yet. It must know roughly where I am. What is it waiting for? Why doesn't it just take a chance? At worst, it will miss its mark.

Then I notice its hide isn't decorated with sores alone, but with scars too.

It doesn't know whether I am a man or a bear. To make a mistake with me would be no terrible thing, but to misjudge its attack upon a bear or balegoat could see it badly injured, perhaps mortally so. It is a pitiable thing, and pitiable things always learn patience.

It takes another step forward. Another calm, patient step.

One more and I will run. I know I will.

Then the Lady Blackbelly—the same and greedy or another—leaps from the water once more.

The scabwolf's head snaps right again, green-yellow slobber swinging from its slack jaws.

I slide the arrow out and notch it in a single motion as my father has taught me.

And the scabwolf hears the sound, its head lashing back toward me, lips pulled back to reveal red, raw gums.

I draw the bow and the creature leaps. It is as if I have it on a leash, yanking it toward me.

I let the arrow fly, then dart right.

But the ground is slippy—I would never have made it up the riverbank, Five Feathers or not—and sprawl in the mud, losing the bow and cracking my chin on a stone.

I am up again in a flash, spitting blood, my hand reaching for my knife, forgetting the sword.

The scabwolf is lying on its side, my arrow buried in its shoulder, good and deep, at least half the shaft hidden in its sour flesh, blood bubbling up around the wood.

At last, I swallow and take a proper breath.

Not taking my eyes from the fallen beast—it is still breathing, shallow and ragged, but breathing nonetheless—I retrieve my bow. The wood *clacks* against a stone.

And the scabwolf is up and lurching toward me.

This time I run. Up the bank and away, not slipping once. Later I will tell myself it was a logical choice—the thing was wounded and so would be slower, less likely to catch me—but it is fear that propels me, make no mistake.

I run up into the woods, away from the scabwolf, away from the river and the Lady Blackbelly. I lose track of how long I run and in which direction. I only stop running when I realise it is getting dark.

Surely I haven't been running *that* long.

I look up. No, it isn't dark. The canopy above me is dense, allowing in little light. Gesneh trees. They are tall and dark, their trunks a near-black red. The low branches are stubby and leafless, the high ones heavy with thick leaves, the size of a man's face. The leaves are used for dyeing clothes.

But only the Jarl and his cronies are permitted to wear red.

Then I remember something else about gesneh trees. Moss will not grow on them.

"Ged!" I shout. "Idiot! Gedding idiot!"

I take a deep breath, calm myself.

With no moss to navigate, I am lost.

I look to the next tree and the next, and the next. And every one is a gesneh tree.

I am about to launch into another tirade of self-reproach liberally peppered with the kind of words that would have seen me on the receiving end of my mother's palm only a year or so back when I realise I only need to find the sun to know which direction to go. It must be getting close to end-of-day now, and the sun sets in the west. I only need to find the sun and head in something like the opposite direction.

I scale the nearest tree easily, the stubby low branches as good as the rungs of any ladder. In just a few seconds, I am up among the high branches, surrounded by leaves the colour of the Jarl's ceremonial cloak, the one he wore when he inflicted the Seven Cuts upon me. The *eight* cuts, I remind myself. That last one, the seventh, across the thighs, was a monstrous cheat. Just as quickly as I ascend into the canopy, I locate the sun off to my right. It is not as late as I thought. It has perhaps two hours to go before it finds the horizon.

I am about to climb back down when I hear the whistling of a grefa stone.

Close by.

Very close by.

Chapter 6

The Boy I Kissed

I wedge myself against the trunk, unshoulder my bow and nock an arrow.

The whistling is getting louder.

And there are voices. Two of them.

"It will be quicker if we split up, Father."

"Oh, yes, what a tremendous idea, Dwynan. Yes, let's split up. A fine plan."

"So pleased you agree with me for once, Father. It is a fine plan, is it not?"

"It will be a good experience for you, lad. It will build character, as a straggis wasp builds its conical house from animal hair and mud."

"Indeed, Father, a grand experience. What could provide a better experience for a boy of sixteen than finding himself lost among the gesneh trees? I can already feel my character improving. Why, my character is measurably better than it was just three steps ago. I suspect my character will soon be so big it might topple over, a victim of its own greatness."

I realise then that it is not two voices, but one talking to itself. What's more, I recognise that voice and the name it spoke of.

Dwynan.

Dwynan Furral.

We kissed once, a year ago, behind the Jarl's stable, during the Festival of Seros. His lips were soft, and he tasted of yellowberries.

Before we kissed, he spoke to me often. After, not at all.

He steps into view then, the grefa stone held out ahead of him in his palm. Its whistling is suddenly so high it is like the shrieking of a scalded infant. He tugs his sword from his scabbard. Or tries to. It takes him three attempts to free the blade. He turns on the spot, seeking out the Glyster who must be somewhere very close by for the stone to be behaving so. He looks everywhere but up.

"Hello?" he says, his voice tremulous with fear. "Show yourself, Glystgedder. Prepare to… meet… you know… your doom and all that. At the point of my sword and what have you."

I try not to laugh.

And then I realise there is nothing to laugh about.

I cannot let him see me. Because, if he sees me, I will have to kill him. I cannot let him go back to the Jarl and nay-say my father's account. That would be death for my father.

I draw my bowstring, training the arrow's point on Dwynan's chest.

He shoves the grefa stone into a pouch on his belt, gripping the sword with both hands. Then he proceeds to work his way through the most basic sword drills, the simple kind my father taught me immediately I was well enough after the Ritual.

He is not very good. There is every chance I will not have to kill him because he will do the job himself with a slip of the blade.

I try not to laugh again. Then I remind myself of the seriousness of the situation. I have never killed a man before. Of course I haven't. In fact, I have only ever seen a man die at another man's hands once.

We were hunting, my father and I, not far from where the events of today took a turn for the worse. We had already bagged two welpa and had found enough honey mushrooms for a month of soups. There was plenty of light left, and my father was considering setting a snare before we headed home. If we were lucky, we might return in the morning to find a foorstig or, if we were very lucky, a kanna. But luck is a bucket with a hole. The moment my father knelt down to begin work on the snare, two men rushed into the clearing. They were as big as my father, but not solid like him. They were wiry, grimy and desperate. One held a sword that looked like it had been pillaged from a barrow, the other an axe that was made for felling small trees, not men. And certainly not men like my father, who had battled against the Sceada when they had attempted to sack Brim, back when I was still in my cot.

My father was up in an instant, his sword drawn before he was even upright. He strode toward his attackers. The axeman fell first, not even afforded the opportunity to raise his weapon. I didn't even see where he was struck it happened so quickly. The second man realised his mistake and turned to run. My father's sword carved through the meat of the man's neck and shoulder, releasing a mist of blood. The man let out a sound, half whine, half grunt, and fell face first. My father plunged his sword deep into the man's back, high up, so as to find his heart. Then he returned to the axeman, gurgling on his back, and found his heart too.

It was all done in seconds.

When my heart had stopped erupting, I said, "Is it not wrong to put a sword into a man's back, Father?"

He shook his head.

"In a duel, yes. Possibly in battle, too. But not when fighting men such as this. Not when there could be more of them skulking in the Freewood. He could have gone to them and brought them to us. No. Sometimes what must be done, must be done."

"We are nowhere other than here," I said, quoting my mother.

My father smiled.

"Yes. Precisely that. We are nowhere other than here."

I look down now, at scared, hopeless Dwynan. *We are nowhere other than here.*

I draw my bowstring back until it is anchored.

But I can't seem to let the arrow fly. I just train it on Dwynan as he continues to turn on the spot, having to change my target as he revolves: chest, back, neck.

And then he stops turning, and I know he has finally considered the possibility that his quarry has scuttled upward. Fortunately, his back is to me as he scans the first of the gesneh trees. But he is slowly tracking round toward my tree, toward my crow's nest.

I will have to kill him. What choice do I have?

But this is not a scabwolf or a welpa. It is a man. A boy, really. A boy I kissed behind the stables at the Festival of Seros. A boy whose soft lips tasted of yellowberries. A boy who before that kiss, used to talk to me about his plans to build a boat and fish off the coast at Brim and live in a house near the shore. He was a good fisherman as I remember, bringing back many Lady Blackbellies, whitecollars and, once, a rumpfish that was almost as big as him.

But what choice do I have?

I take a breath and hold it.

Release the breath, release the arrow, I hear my father say.

And then the leak-sprung bucket of luck favours me.

The scabwolf, my arrow still protruding from its shoulder like the spine of a tindhog, lumbers into view, snarling and slobbering.

The beast captures the entirety of Dwynan's attention.

He drops the sword, turns and runs.

The scabwolf lurches after him.

Its wound has slowed it considerably, and it is unlikely to catch him. But that is between Dwynan and the scabwolf, and not my business.

I listen to the muffled whistling of the grefa stone fading into the distance, then I make my way down the tree. I am about to set off eastward when a violent trembling overtakes me. I only have to wonder about the cause for a moment or two.

I nearly killed someone. I nearly put an arrow into someone, another person. A person like me. It would be a Changing Thing, such an act. It would have altered me as surely as the Ritual of the Seven Cuts and the Seven Cups. But I am not sure how.

I am certain of one thing, however. Such an act, the taking of a life, sits somewhere in my future. Somewhere close by.

The trembling subsides and I head east.

After half a mile or so, I find my way clear of the gesneh trees, and I hear the sound of the River Woever off to my right. I am back on track. For the next two hours, I make good progress and do not hear a single grefa stone. But the light begins to fade, and I know I must find somewhere to bed down for the night.

The hollow trunk of a dead oak provides a reasonable shelter, with just enough space for me to sit, though I desperately wish to lie down. I desperately wish for my own bed in my own roundhouse, but wishes, as my mother would say, cannot mend a sock. I wrap myself in my father's cloak and, doing my best to ignore the various scuttling bugs and the smell of damp and rot, I try to sleep.

I must have succeeded because I dream I am in the Jarl's squarehouse. I dream of my father.

No... I dream I *am* my father.

The Jarl jabs a finger at me from his tall gesnehwood chair.

"Liar!" he shouts. "Liar! Your child is the Glystgedder! Admit it!"

"No," I say, my voice calm despite the tumult of emotions churning inside me. Sadness, fear, rage, panic. "It is not so. It is as I told you. We saw a man who made fire with his hands. It was he who set the grefa stones to whistling. We gave chase, and I lost sight of both the man and my Alys."

"That is a lie!" The Jarl rises from his chair and strides toward me. His hand hovers near the hilt of his sword, and mine, without being bid, does likewise.

I could kill the Jarl, I think. Or my father thinks. It is unclear whose thoughts are whose.

He is no threat to me, the Jarl. He has drunk too much mead these last few years, eaten too much good meat from the Tanwood, and far too many of the huge round potatoes that grow in the rich soil on its periphery. His middle is like an overfilled waterskin, and his eyes, like his wits, are dull.

But if I strike him down, his men will be upon me in moments, and I will not survive the onslaught. I am certain that I would be able to take two or three of them with me, but not all. And though I must pretend my Alys is lost to me, I know a day may come—in fact, I feel certain a day will come—when she will need me.

I force my hand away from my sword.

"It is as I told you, Jarl. I swear it."

The Jarl growls, spins on his heel and strides back to his chair. He sits and glares at me for a full minute.

"I believe you not, Clainh. I. Believe. You. *Not*."

"It is as I said. There was a man—"

The Jarl roars. And despite his waterskin belly and lightless eyes, I experience a quiver of fear.

Then, in a whisper, he says, "If I find you are lying, I will cut off your hands and put out your eyes and send you down to the Woever where the scabwolves skulk. And you *are* lying. And I *will* find you out."

I cease to be afraid of the Jarl at that moment. I am thinking about the Woever and the scabwolves and how I hadn't had time to remind little Alys of their strengths and weaknesses.

The Jarl brings me back to myself with a yell of, "Slek! Slek Mydra!"

The name fills me with dread. Me and my father both.

Footsteps approach. I turn and Slek Mydra is standing in the doorway. He is six and a half feet tall and broad as a bear. He is wearing the blood-red leather of the Sceada and his head is shaved, as is the fashion of the men from across the sea.

"Yes, my Jarl," he says in that always unexpectedly soft voice of his.

Mydra was captured during one of Gafol's run-ins with the men from Scead. He won his freedom in the Trial of Suswylt, the scars from which decorate his face and arms. The Jarl calls him 'Brother' now, and there is nothing Mydra will not do for the Jarl.

"Find Clainh's brat," says the Jarl. "Bring her to me. If the grefa stone whistles, put your sword to her and bring me her corpse."

"It is already so," says Mydra in that almost soothing voice of his.

It is already so. A Scead expression which means: I am so confident I can carry out your instructions that, at some point in the future, the deed is done.

I snap awake in the tree hollow and, for a lingering instant, I am both my father fearing for his daughter and his daughter fearing for her father. I am he and I am I.

Somewhere in the night, a spider owl cries out, and I count backwards from ten, as the old wives' tale says we must, to undo its death curse.

Sleep does not find me again.

Chapter 7

A Choice of Deaths

As soon as the sun is peering over the horizon, I am up and heading east. I make good progress, reaching the bridge in a little over an hour.

The bridge.

It is hardly deserving of the name.

It is missing more planks than an old man's mouth lacks teeth, and greenery has gathered to it as to the hide of a slite. It looks like it would struggle to accept the weight of a water mouse, let alone mine. I consider finding somewhere the river is not so wide and swift, somewhere I might cross, but I remember stories of the snakefish that coil about the stones on the riverbed, their bite so poisonous it turns flesh to liquid in less than a day. It is said the victim of a snakefish bite cannot be burned on a death pyre, as is honourable, because they cannot burn. Their remains are too wet. They can only be poured into a hole in the ground, far from where the crops grow and the animals feed.

No. It is the bridge or nothing.

I place one foot on the deck.

It groans. A deep, throaty sound.

I take a breath.

Calm, I tell myself. *Appraise the situation.*

The bridge is about a hundred yards across, perhaps less. Which means I can be at the far side in fewer than a hundred strides. Taking it slow and steady, I will be across in just a minute or two.

I place my other foot on the bridge, and the old wood groans again.

I start to walk, taking long purposeful strides.

I am only eight strides in when I reach the first gap. I look down to the fast-moving waters of the Woever. It is only a drop of some twenty feet. I fell from a tree not much under that when I was nine. But there were branches to slow my descent, and the ground upon which I landed was mossy. It knocked the wind out of me for what felt like forever, but I received no permanent injuries and was back to climbing trees the next day. There would be nothing to slow my descent if I were to fall from the bridge. And though there is doubtless some greenery on the bottom of the river, it clings to a bed of rocks and stones. And then there are the snakefish to consider.

The gap is perhaps a stride-and-a-half wide. A short leap, one foot forward, and I'll be over.

But what of the wood at my landing point? Where it is not green with lichen and moss, it is sickly pale, like the ball mushrooms me and Roisa would poke with a stick to watch the air fill with their glittering spores.

I sidle left and right, looking for a spot where the wood is not quite so *fungal*.

Finding the least unsatisfactory destination, I unburden myself of my bow, quiver, waterskin, knife, sword, game sack and my father's cloak, and toss them across the gap.

Then I leap.

The wood does not groan when I land. It *squeals.* And then it cracks.

But I am already skipping two steps forward to a sturdier spot.

I realise I have stopped breathing and give myself leave to start again.

I gather my things and carry on.

Twice more I tackle such gaps in the bridge's structure, and each time the wood squeals at me and cracks, and I skip away to a place where the wood looks like wood and not the flesh of a mushroom.

The fourth gap I encounter, at just over the bridge's halfspan, is almost twice as wide as the others I have crossed.

I will have to jump with both feet. I will almost certainly land heavily. And none of the wood on the other side looks like wood. It all has the quality of a particularly ripe ball mushroom, the flesh of which sometimes collapses in *anticipation* of the prod of a twig.

Perhaps if I roll as I land? Or quickly flatten myself, spreadeagled?

As if to dissuade me from further prevarication, I hear—distant but distinct—the whistling of a grefa stone. The men of Gafol are up early as bedwetters and searching for me. Hunting me.

"Ged!"

I have to move quickly now. I am out in the open here on the bridge. A good marksman could pick me off with an arrow from the treeline. What's more, I can be seen. I can be recognised. Even if I escape, word will get back to the Jarl that it was Alys Clainh, daughter and son of Aryc Clainh, who set the grefa stones to whistling.

If I find you are lying, I will cut off your hands and put out your eyes and send you down to the Woever where the scabwolves skulk. And you are *lying. And I* will *find you out.*

I remove my belongings and toss them across the gap.

Then I jump.

Where my heels strike the deck, it is greased with lichen, and my feet fly out from beneath me. My lower back strikes the soft, fungal wood. My shoulders strike nothing and my head flops back into the hole over which I have just leapt. I am afforded a view of the underside of the bridge, then the riverbank, then the racing waters. I snatch at wood with panicked hands, fingers sinking into the rot, anchoring me in place. Splinters, somehow soft *and* sharp, slide beneath my fingernails. The pain is disproportionate to the size of the wounds inflicted.

Slowly, I pull myself back up. Very slowly. I know that if I am too hasty, I will pull the rotted wood away in handfuls. I see the riverbank again. At this horribly slow pace, I see the red caitlins that grow near the water's edge, and the redder ember butterflies that feed upon them. Then I see the underside of the bridge once more. And wish I hadn't.

Beneath the deck are the remains of a criss-crossing structure of supporting joists. It is no longer capable of supporting much of anything, hanging away in places like a sagging net. The joists are studded with pale-yellow cones, about six inches high. I recognise them immediately because I have been taught to be wary of them. Nests. Straggis wasp nests. Perhaps as many as fifty of the things stretching back to the start of the bridge, and who knows how many glued to the bottom of the rest of its span? The nearest nest is an arm's length from my face, close enough that I can see the enquiring antenna of its occupant testing the air, can hear its low, threatening drone.

I take a breath and hold it.

Straggis wasps are attracted to something in the air we expel from our lungs. Nobody knows what. Some say they can sense the tiny portion of soul we exhale with each used breath.

I am not cautious in dragging myself up now. Fear has the better of me.

The wood into which my right hand is sunk comes away, like meat from a slow-cooked pig. But the left hand remains anchored, and soon I am up on the deck gasping in air.

I gather my things and start forward again and see that every gap in the deck between me and the far riverbank is as wide, if not wider, than the one I only just managed to leap.

And the whistling of the grefa stones is getting louder. In fact, I think I can hear voices too. Someone singing. A hunting song? I think I recognise it. I judge that I have only a minute or two to get across before whoever it is singing— badly—discovers me.

If I can't trust the deck or the joists, what of the beams that run parallel down either side of the bridge? I make my way to the left-hand side. The beam is the length of the entire bridge and, with no pier supporting it—not even at the halfspan—it must be strong. I cannot fathom what kind of tree it was cut from. It would have to have been at least three hundred feet tall while it lived. And it does not sag, not in the least. Perhaps something from the time of the Abundance? Perhaps something made with the Glyst.

However it came to be, it is clearly strong. But it is narrow, not much more than the width of my foot. I step onto it. It doesn't groan. With my arms held out straight on either side of me, I start forward.

It is easy going for the most part, the remnants of the deck making up for the beam's lack of width. And the intervals where the deck has rotted or fallen away completely are covered within just six or seven steps. I am feeling quite pleased with myself. Until I have just ten yards to go and see that there is no deck at all for that remaining stretch. It's just a beam. Narrow beam.

I don't recall consciously deciding to stop moving, and yet I am suddenly motionless. I tell myself not to look down and then do precisely that. There is more riverbank than water beneath me, scattered with rocks and clusters of spear-like gawgrass.

Dizziness threatens. I force myself to look straight ahead and concentrate on placing one foot in front of the other.

"This is no difficult thing," I tell myself. Once a troupe of performers had come to Gafol. They had eaten fire, juggled, and one of them, a skinny man with the palest flesh, had walked a rope drawn tight from the roof of the Jarl's squarehouse to the gaddapole at the centre of our village. He had made it look easy, the skinny man. A beam of solid wood, as much as ten times the width of a rope, should present no problems.

And then I hear the deep drone of a straggis wasp. I cannot see it, only hear it. Somewhere close by, and getting closer, getting louder.

I find myself motionless once more.

Over the drone of the wasp, the whistling of a grefa stone—or stones?—and a fragment of hunting song:

> *We will catch it and skin it*
> *We will cure it and cut it*
> *We will stitch it and wear it*
> *Our prey, our prey*
> *This will be a good day!*

I take two steps forward and the wasp makes its appearance, gliding into view from over my right shoulder and passing me by so close I feel the wind from its wings, and its drone drowns out the hunting song. Its black and yellow body is as large as that of a swallow. Its stinger, curved and barbed, is fully extended, more than half the length of its body.

I hold my breath.

The wasp continues on, away from me.

Then pauses in its flight, as I am paused on this too-narrow beam.

It pivots in the air and floats toward me.

I can hear the hunting song over its drone now.

Our prey, our prey
This will be a good day!

The wasp hovers an inch from my face at eye level. It is so close it is just a blur of black and yellow. And then it lands on my face, scuttling across my cheek, over my ear and up into my hair, its legs like supple twigs.

I almost cry out.

The venom of the straggis wasp, in very small doses, can be used to lessen pain. In slightly larger doses, it can deaden a limb so completely that limb can be removed. As when Clod Ashling had the bloodrot in his leg. A full dose kills so quickly it is said there is no time for the soul to leave the body.

This will be a good day!
This will be a good day!

I judge that I have less than a minute before I am seen. I have a choice between an arrow between the shoulder blades, a brutal fall to the rocks below or the very real possibility of a sting from a straggis wasp. This is not a good day.

Dripping sweat burns my eyes, my lungs ache from holding my breath and my heart is punching at my chest, trying to escape.

But in the end, there is only one choice. If I am seen, my father dies. I have to get across the bridge and out of sight, and I have to do it now.

Just as I stopped moving without telling myself to do so, I am moving again without instruction. I move with the ease of the pale, skinny man on his rope, despite the scratching of the wasp's legs on my scalp.

This will be a good day!

I am thinking that it might, indeed, be a good day, after all. The end of the bridge is just three steps away when the wasp stings me.

Chapter 8

Arrows and Spears

I do not die, instantly or otherwise.

The wasp stings me again.

Still, I do not die.

I am wondering if the Glyst that allowed me to bring my father back from death has made me immune to its venom. Perhaps to all venoms. Perhaps to death itself.

Then I remember I have experienced this stinging pain before. When the other children and I were being taught our scripts, sat on the floor in Mrs Blathnyd's roundhouse, and that idiot boy, Keary Morr, sat behind me, had taken to pulling single hairs from my head. And I remember what Dwynan said as he passed beneath my tree, pretending to be his father.

It will be a good experience for you, lad. It will build character, as a straggis wasp builds its conical house from animal hair and mud.

Its building materials pillaged, the straggis wasp lifts from my head and drones off back the way it came.

I leap the remaining distance onto the good, firm ground of the riverbank. Without pausing to enjoy the warm rush of relief that surges through me, I dart into a dense patch of red caitlins and make myself small.

"There!" a voice cries out from across the river, competing with the high whistle of a grefa stone. "Look! There!"

The rush of relief is replaced by a sudden frost of dread.

But I'm sure I can't be seen. The caitlins are tall, with leafy stems, and grow in thick clusters. I should be well hidden.

"There!"

I turn slowly on the spot so I am looking back toward the bridge and whoever it is that appears to have spotted me.

"Look!" he says.

It is Eltas, the butcher. That is not a warrior name. He is not Eltas the Butcher. He is Eltas, the butcher. His name is Eltas and he is the Jarl's butcher, preparing his meat for storing or cooking. With him is his brother, Eftas. Eftas hasn't the skill to be a butcher. He is a slaughter man. They are almost indistinguishable from one another, the Hilder brothers. Both bald, both wide, both with the same piggy faces.

Eltas seems to be pointing directly at me.

"There!" he says. "Butterflies!"

I tip my head back by degrees until I am looking upward. A cloud of ember butterflies. I must have scattered them when I scuttled into hiding. They signal my whereabouts as surely as a campfire made with greenwood.

"I see them," says Eftas. He takes his bow from his back then selects and nocks an arrow.

"It is too far, you idiot," says Eltas.

"It is not," says Eftas and looses the arrow.

It strikes the deck of the bridge a good forty yards short of where I leapt to safety.

"See," says Eltas. "I told you."

"Shut up," says Eftas, and makes his way to the start of the bridge. He takes two steps onto the deck. Then two steps off. "It's soft as pudding," he says and nocks another arrow.

"What are you shooting at?" says Eltas. "It's not as if we can see anything. Could be anything set those embers to flight. A fox or a rat. Could be anything."

"And what of the stone?" says Eftas. "It's whistling, is it not?"

Eltas looks at the stone in his palm and says, "The gedding thing hasn't stopped whistling since yesterday!" He shoves it deep down into his side bag, muffling the sound.

Eftas trains his arrow in my approximate direction and looses his arrow.

It strikes the ground several yards to the right of me and a good ten yards from where the caitlins begin.

"I'm sure I see something," he says. "Squatting, Low down." He nocks another arrow.

"Well, that rules out the Clainh girl," says Eltas. "No way she'd have made it this far. Not with the scabwolves and the snakefish. No way she'd have crossed that bridge, either. Look at it. I've seen sturdier carcasses in the height of summer."

Eftas looses another arrow. It strikes closer this time, only a couple of yards to my right, and only five yards from the caitlins.

"She could have walked along the outer beam," says Eftas. "Balancing, like. Remember when those players came from Claefol, and that man who was the colour of a ghost walked on a rope from the Jarl's place to the gaddapole?"

"I remember," says Eltas. "But I doubt the girl would possess the guts for such a task."

Eftas selects another arrow.

I begin to shuffle backwards. I can't risk just waiting for the next arrow to land. It would probably miss, but I can't be sure. And I'm confident they cannot see me.

"Look!" shouts Eltas. "The caitlins are moving. If that's you, girl, stay put. We will not hurt you."

"Not to begin with, anyway," says Eftas in the tone of voice I have heard men use when they have too much mead in them.

Eltas laughs. "Come on. Show yourself."

Eftas releases the arrow.

I continue to shuffle backwards.

The arrow lands inches from where I was just squatting. I don't *think* it would have struck me.

"Come on, girl!" shouts Eftas. "We needn't put a hole in you. Let us see you! Last chance." He nocks an arrow.

Then Eltas, his voice almost as high as the whistle of a grefa stone, says, "Wasps!"

"What?" says Eftas.

"Wasps! Straggis wasps!"

Eftas drops his bow, turns and runs. Likewise, Eltas.

I watch as they disappear back into the Freewood, waving their hands around their heads and wailing.

Once the Hilder brothers' voices have faded completely, I head out onto the road the bridge once served. It has been made narrow by overgrowth and is pocked with craters such that you have to watch your footing or risk a wrenched or broken ankle.

It takes a full mile of walking for my nerves to calm from the events of the bridge, and when they do I am suddenly aware of just how hungry I am. My belly is an empty cave, haunted by the growls of a long-dead bear. If I were a complete fool, I'd get a fire going, skin and cook the welpa. But I am not a complete fool. I am only half a fool, so I pick some berries from the scraggy bushes that line the road. They look a little like yellowberries, except they are smaller and not so juicy. They do not taste like yellowberries, but they are pleasant enough. I do not eat many. Just enough to silence the growling in my belly-cave. The growling is replaced by my father's chiding voice.

Child, you must never eat a thing unless you know what that thing is. The land does not repay stupidity with kindness.

If I was not so hungry, I might have heard my father's voice *before* I ate the berries. But hunger has a way of silencing good sense.

As I walk, I brace myself for the doubtless inevitable stomach cramps or, worse, a sudden and uncontrollable wateriness in the bowels. For two hours I steel myself, but the cramp and the wateriness do not come. The land has repaid my stupidity with, if not kindness, a neutral nod of its head.

The bushes with their not-yellowberries thin out and fields of thick grasses fall away on either side of me. To my right, I think I can make out the low undulations of the Scoddy Hills, on the far side of which is Brim and then the rough waters of the Benna Sea. To my left, perhaps seven or eight miles distant, is the Forest of Leccan, beyond which the Beorstehd Mountains are vast and jagged, the Seven Peaks snagging at the grey-black blanket of rain-heavy cloud that is making its way toward me at some considerable speed.

I was lucky with the berries, but I do not think I am going to be so lucky with the weather.

The sky favours me for another hour, then seems to unburden itself of every drop of water in a five-minute downpour that, with nowhere for me to shelter, soaks me to the skin. I have never seen rain like it. It falls in arrows and spears, and soon the old path is a rushing brook, and I am not walking but wading,

With the mud sucking at my feet, my legs, already tired, begin to ache. Likewise my neck and shoulders as I hunch against the cold and the wet. Misery soaks my soul as surely as the rain soaks my clothes.

Count the good until one hand is full, I hear my mother say.

"One," I say. "The scabwolf did not take me."

I extend the thumb of my right hand.

"Two," I say. "Dwynan did not see me, so my father shall live."

I extend my first finger.

"Three. The straggis wasp did not sting me."

I extend my second finger.

"Four. The idiot Hilder brothers did not land an arrow in my hide."

I extend my third finger.

"Five. The not-yellowberries did not turn my bowels to water and have me ged myself like a mewling puke-baby."

I extend my little finger.

"I have a full hand of good," I say. "And that is well and fine."

I hear my mother say it, too.

I have a full hand of good. And that is well and fine.

"And that is well and fine," I echo.

As if to reward my gratitude, the rain begins to ease off a touch. It is just heavy rain now and not an assault of water.

Trees begin to appear at the roadside. Just a scattering to begin with but gathering over the next mile until there is forest on either side of me. The rain on the leaves is loud and heavy, bending the younger branches until it seems as if the woods are full of movement. Full of things.

I draw my father's sword.

A few feet into the forest to my left, something snakes down the trunk of a fat, old tree. But it is just rainwater, trickling in thick glistening ropes. To my right, there is a clatter, and I see a huge nedercrow disappear up into the darkening canopy. Behind me, something splashes. I spin round so fast I almost lose the sword. But there is nothing there.

I am jumping at nothings. Rainwater and crows and nothings.

I should sheath the sword. A drawn sword with no enemy in view can summon trouble, it is said. I have had enough trouble for one day. More than enough.

The moment the sword is housed in its scabbard, the air a few yards in front of me seems to ripple, as if a wind is blowing through the rain. But I feel no wind.

And then the rain parts like a curtain.

And the very air tears open, as when a long cut with a sharp knife opens a fish's belly and the wound spreads to release the creature's guts and makes you wonder how they all fit inside its body in the first place.

But there are no fish guts pushing from this wound, this wound in the air. There is nothing. Just a darkness that seems to go on forever. It seems to have a weight and a texture, that darkness. It feels as if that darkness is not simply the lack of light, as when a candle is extinguished, but—and I not only feel this to be so, I *know* it to be so—the darkness is what becomes of light when it is bled-out and dead. The darkness, this very particular darkness that lies beyond the wound in in the air, is *murdered* light.

And then something… *something* is striding toward me from out of that darkness, that carcass of light.

It is just as my mother described it.

Tall and thin and white, with too many joints in its limbs. Its head is long and fleshless, and where a mouth should be are tentacles as of the squid that can be netted at Brim.

The tentacles begin to grow, stretching toward me, floating as hair floats on water.

It is wrapped in strips of the darkness from which it came. It is bandaged in murdered light.

Cwalee.

Chapter 9

The Man with Burning Hands

I draw my sword, staggering back, away from the Cwalee's questing tendrils. They are like bloodless worms, but thick and long. Getting longer. At the tapered end of each worm is something like a puckered mouth, opening and closing, ringed with tiny, black teeth.

My foot sinks into a mud-filled hole. I try to pull it free while maintaining my retreat, and I fall backwards, splashing down into the rainwater. My ankle ignites with pain and my elbow strikes something hard. The sword is jolted from my hand. I quest for it, but I cannot take my eyes from the thing that is now striding toward me, the Cwalee, and my fingers find only water and mud and stones.

It looms over me now, its tentacles dangling.

Its long skull is not fleshless; rather, its flesh is as thin as that of a single onion layer and as transparent. There are inscriptions, either on the flesh or the bone beneath, in a pale blue ink. They are like no script I have ever been shown by Mrs Blathnyd. It turns its head a little to the side, inspecting me with one eye. It is the yellow of an untreated wound, that eye, and the pupil is not round like ours. It is a red triangle. It is the eye from the Jarl's bowl of grefa stones.

The tentacles descend toward me.

My hand finds the sword. I grip it and swing. The Cwalee leaps back.

"What the gedding hell do you think you're doing, idiot child?" it snaps.

It has the voice of a woman. A very irate woman.

It shakes its head, tentacles swinging in time.

"You've been at the gesithberries, haven't you? Idiot. I thought your father would have taught you better than that."

I swing the sword again.

"Put that thing down. You'll more likely injure yourself than me."

And, suddenly, there is no Cwalee, and no wound filled with murdered light hanging in the air. There is a woman—a very irate woman—standing in the road with her arms folded. She has the look of my father. Something in the eyes and the set of the mouth.

"Aunty Elsam?"

I drop the sword.

"Yes, Alys. What the ged are you doing out here? And eating gesithberries like a simpleton."

Now that the sword is down, she walks toward me, kneels at my side.

"You've got your foot stuck in a hole, child," she says. "How d'you manage that? Honestly, I've met brighter scabwolves."

She eases the foot out of the hole in the road. My ankle shrieks with pain and I cry out.

"Oh, stop it," says Aunty Elsam. "It's just a bit of pain, little fussbaby. If you don't like it, you shouldn't have put your foot in a hole in the first place. You should watch what you're doing and where you're going, that's what you should do. And eating *gesithberries*? And—"

She reaches across me and picks up the sword. She balances it in her hand. There is an ease with which she does this that tells me she is more than capable of putting it to good use.

"Why do you have Aryc's sword?" she says. "Is your father… has he passed?"

"No," I say, then look away. "But Mammy has."

"Oh," she says, and her voice is soft. "I liked her. I liked her a lot. Too good for that idiot little brother of mine." She slides a hand round my waist and lifts me. "Let's get you inside and warm and dry."

Her roundhouse is as my father had said it would be: set back from the road, in a carved-out clearing in the woods, concealed by a thick growth of thornbushes at the roadside. It is a house that does not wish to be found, and I suspect I would have walked right past it.

It is neat and simple inside. The circular hearthstone in the middle of the house has a strong fire going, and there is a pot suspended over it in which something delicious-smelling simmers. There is a chair next to the hearth and, off to one side, a bed covered in heavy furs and woollen blankets. On the opposite side to the bed is a collection of earthenware pots and a small table with two chairs. Herbs and drying meats hang from the ceiling there. On the far side from where we entered the roundhouse is what I can only describe as an armoury. Swords, shields, bows, arrows, helmets and mismatched pieces of armour are arranged in an ordered fashion against the wall.

"Sit," says Aunty Elsam, pointing to the chair.

She goes to a wicker hamper at the foot of her bed and pulls out a tunic, trousers, a cloak, all in the darkest green.

"Here," she says, handing them to me. "Get out of those wet things and into these. The stew is almost done."

While I change, she attends to the pot. By the time I am dressed, she has two bowls of stew ready and hands me one, then a wooden spoon.

She sits on the edge of the hearth.

I am scraping my bowl clean while hers is still almost half full. Other than goat and mushrooms, I don't recognise any of the flavours. That said, the food is not on my tongue long enough for me to make much of an assessment.

"When did you last eat?" she asks. "Other than the gesithberries."

"Yesterday morning, before we left for the hunt, me and my father."

She nods, then says, "Tell me everything."

I tell her of the slite, my father's mortal wound, the Glyst, the scabwolf, Dwynan Furral, the bridge, the straggis wasps and the Hilder brothers.

By the end of my telling, there is no mistaking the look on her face. Anger. I wonder what I have done to upset her, and as she stands from the hearth, placing her bowl aside, I shrink back into the chair, fearing the worst.

"Those gedding idiots," she says. "Ten years I have been gone, and in that time the folk of Gafol have grown no wiser. The Glyst is a danger to nobody. Not while it is scattered about, a few people here and there. The Cwalee came because of the Maradyns and their schools and cities. The Cwalee came because of the dense clusters of Glyst, as a hornwhale is drawn to a shoal of fish but ignores the solitary swimmers. The Glyst is a great blessing, especially a Glyst such as yours.

The Jarl could eradicate sickness from the village and trade your gift with other villages, exchanging it for food and tools and garments. Instead, he would put you to the sword. Gedding idiot."

She is pacing now, her hands clenched into fists.

Ten years? I think. She has been gone ten years.

"Noola Fynn," I say.

And Aunty Elsam stops pacing.

"What?" she says.

"That was ten years ago. Noola Fynn. I was six. I was six when I first heard the grefa stones and my father came home smelling of blood."

She sits at the hearth again and stares down at her hands as they clutch at each other in her lap.

"I tried to stop him. I tried to tell him about the man with burning hands."

"The man with burning hands?" I remember what my father said before we parted in the Freewood:

I'll tell them we saw someone in the Freewood, a man. A man making fire with his bare hands. A man with the Glyst. I'll say we chased him and he escaped, but after that I could not find you. I will make a pretence of searching for you for the rest of my life. And they will believe me, because my face will be a mask of sorrow until I die.

And then later when I dreamed I was him as I slept in the tree-hollow:

It is as I told you. We saw a man who made fire with his hands. It was he who set the grefa stones to whistling. We gave chase, and I lost sight of both the man and my Alys.

"Yes," my aunty continues. "I saw him on the edge of the Freewood. I was a little younger than you. I shouldn't really have been that far from home, but where the Freewood meets the fenland, the soil is dark and rich and yields the finest mushrooms. I'd gathered a good sackful and was about to head back because the sun was dropping low, when I saw him. He wasn't much older than me, but he was grubby looking and ill-fed. He was making a fire, placing the wood and the kindling with the care of a small child trying to build the tallest pebble tower on the shore at Brim. But then, instead of using tinder and a flint, he just... *clicked* his fingers." She clicks her own fingers to demonstrate. "And suddenly his hand was gloved in flame. He held his fingers to the kindling until it was burning steadily, then he *shook* his hand." She shakes her own hand. "As you would if you were flicking away a beadybug that was crawling across your knuckles. And the fire vanished from his hands."

She takes my bowl, fills it with stew, and passes it back to me.

"I should have run back to Gafol," she continues. "I should have run back to Gafol and told them there was a Glyster on the edge of the Freewood, too far for the grefa stones to detect. I should have told them because he was dangerous, this young man with his fire hands. His Glyst would have been calling out in a voice that only the Cwalee could hear, and soon they would come. And not just for the Glyster, but for all of us. For the Cwalee, it is said, are driven mad by the presence of Glyst and are indiscriminate when they rampage. I *should* have told them. But I didn't. He seemed so pitiful, his clothes not much better than rags, as if life had been nothing but hard and cruel to him for all his days. I felt sorry for him. But more than that, when I had seen him make fire with his hand, it had filled me with... *wonder*. It had filled me with a great sense of the bigness of things.

"I was always a difficult child. My mother said I asked too many questions. My father said I went looking for strife. They were both right, of course."

I glance across at the armoury at the back of the roundhouse, and I think of the ease with which she handled my father's sword. Strife, I think.

"The question I was asking then," she says, following my gaze to the armoury and smiling a little, "was why hadn't the Cwalee come for him *already*? It was obvious this wasn't the first time he had called upon the Glyst. The ease with which he'd clicked his fingers and shook the flames from his hand. He must have done this hundreds of times. There was no chance that he'd outfought the Cwalee. He looked like he would have struggled to best a sapling in combat, even if he'd had the high ground. It was possible he might have outwitted them somehow. There was an intelligence to his brow and in his eyes. But I doubted it. How do you outwit insatiable hunger? Some things cannot be defeated by reasoning and intellect. All of which meant the Cwalee simply hadn't bothered with him."

"Because a hornwhale does not bother with the solitary swimmers," I said.

"Yes. Precisely that." She pokes at the fire with an iron rod. "I returned to the edge of the Freewood the next morning. He was sleeping next to the cooling remnants of his campfire. I held a knife to his throat and tapped him on his forehead." She grins. "My word, he almost ged himself! I demanded he tell me everything. About himself and about the Glyst and why the Cwalee had not come for him.

"His name was Madec Teeg. He'd had the Glyst for three years and had been chased from his village near the Leccan Forest. His story shamed me because we had not chased Glysters from our village. We had slain them. Five in my lifetime. He'd been travelling since, one ear always tuned for the whistling of grefa stones. He said he'd met other Glysters during his exile, always in ones and twos, and it was well known among them that the secret to avoiding the attentions of the Cwalee was not to gather in greater numbers than seven. They have a saying, the Glysters. Seven is company, eight a death wish.

"We met every day for a month. He told me about the Glyst and the Glysters, and what he'd learnt of the Maradyns and their schools and cities. I taught him where to find the best mushrooms and how to make a tasty stew with the very herbs that grew near them. I taught him how to make a snare and how he could clean himself with juicy screthleaves so he didn't smell quite so much like a scabwolf. I taught him not to eat gesithberries as they cause waking dreams so real you might ged yourself."

She gives me a stern look, then winks.

"He began to look well, strong even. And then, one day, he was gone. And that was that. I didn't see him again. But from then on, I knew. I knew that the persecution of Glysters was an unnecessary cruelty. That it harmed us more than helped us. That, if we are careful and measured, we could bring back something like the Abundance. I told nobody, though. It was dangerous knowledge that I had. I told nobody until the night of Noola Fynn.

"I saw your father walk past my roundhouse, sword in one hand, whistling grefa stone in the other. And I grabbed him by the scruff and dragged him aside, as I had once when I'd found him about to jab a straggis wasp nest with a long stick. I tried to tell him about Madec and his burning hands. About hornwhales and solitary swimmers. About the Rule of Seven. I tried to tell him the Abundance could return if we were not so cruel and afraid. But he wouldn't listen. And Noola Fynn was put to the sword."

"My father didn't do that," I say, realising I am speaking too quickly but unable to prevent myself. "He said as much to Mammy. It wasn't him."

"No," says Aunty Elsam. "True enough. But he killed the man who was protecting her. He hadn't wanted to, and he was weeping when next he passed my roundhouse. But he cut down Dansk Fynn and so played his part in the death of Noola Fynn."

She pokes the fire again, and I imagine my father as a boy about to poke the straggis wasp nest.

"The next day," says Aunty Elsam, "I left Gafol. I returned only once, a year or so later, to tell your father where he might find me should he ever have need. I was still his big sister. I had a duty. Even if he was an idiot."

She is silent for a while then says, "Right. Let's get this ankle of yours sorted, shall we? And then you should get some sleep. Tomorrow you will need to decide if you are going to stay with me, and help me with my work, or travel to the Dead City."

Chapter 10

The Dead City

Breakfast consists of honeyed oat cakes and goat's milk. Outside, the sun is shining, and it is as if yesterday's torrential rains never fell. My ankle is sore, but I am able to put my weight on it without too much trouble. We have been awake for almost an hour and Aunty Elsam has yet to mention her 'work' or 'the Dead City'. For reasons I cannot fathom, I can't bring myself to ask. Especially about the Dead City.

Then, as if she has somehow spied my thoughts, Aunty Elsam says, "My work is a kind of atonement."

I am sat at the table and she is on the floor next to me, a stone slab in front of her, skinning the welpa my father shot just two days ago. The meat has turned and would make us sick if we were so foolish as to eat it, but the hide might make a reasonable pouch.

"I did not have a hand in the death of Noola Fynn. But I didn't stop it. I don't think I *could* have stopped it. But I think I might have been able to convince my brother to play no part in it, and that would have been something. When I went to see him, that last time, I told him again what Madec

Teeg had told me. I told him about the days I'd spent with Madec without so much as a whiff of the Cwalee. I wasn't sure if he was convinced. But here you are, so my words must have had some weight to them. If I'd invested my words with that same weight ten years ago, he would not have had blood on his hands and shame in his heart. And that is my shame, and it is why I do the work."

"What work, Aunty Elsam?"

She scowls up at me, then points the wicked tip of the fleshing knife in my direction.

"Call me El, for the love of Fryth. Aunty Elsam makes me sound like some dull-eyed frump who thinks only of lost loves and mending socks."

"What work… El?"

She drops the knife, stands and walks over to the collection of earthenware pots off to the side of the table. She takes the lid from the largest pot and begins pulling out old animal skins, worn blankets, torn tunics and trousers, dropping them on the floor. It is only when the pile is half the height of the pot that I hear it. It is dull and seems distant, but it is unmistakable.

The whistling of a grefa stone.

Instinctively, I get up from the table and back away.

Aunty Elsam—El—reaches down into the pot and comes out with a wooden box not much bigger than her hand. It is made of a dark wood and carved with symbols I don't recognise. The whistling is louder now but still surprisingly muted.

She opens the box—the whistling gets louder, louder than I have ever heard it—and takes out the stone. She offers it to me.

I take a few more steps back, shaking my head. "I would rather not."

"Take it, idiot child." She strides toward me, grabs my wrist and pushes the stone into my palm.

I don't know what I expected to happen, but I certainly did not expect it to fall silent. But that's precisely what it does. One moment, whistling. The next, silent.

"I don't know why they do that," says El. "But those that hunt Glysters will use it as a final test. 'When the stone dies,' they say, 'then so must the one who silenced it'."

I examine the grefa stone.

It is a pale green colour, with flecks of white, and there is a hole through its middle. It reminds me of the witchstones that are sometimes found on the shore at Brim. But they are a natural thing, given up by the sea. This looks made by man, the hole drilled through with some tool. It is lighter than I thought it would be, too. It has the weight of something carved from wood.

"You have two options when you hear the whistling of a grefa stone," says El. "Move away from it quickly until you are out of its sight. Or go to it and seize it by any means necessary. Flee it, or silence it. No other choices."

"But why do *you* have one?"

"For my work."

"Which is?"

El takes the grefa stone. I expect it to shriek again, but it doesn't.

"It will not whistle for you again," she says and puts it back in its box and the box back in the pot. "For another Glyster, yes. But not for you." She piles blankets, clothes and rags on top of the box, then places the lid on the pot. For a moment, I think she has either forgotten or chosen to ignore my question. Then she says, "My work? I find Glysters and I help them. I find them, and I take them to places where there are no grefa stones. I teach them what they need to know to fend for themselves. A little of building, a little of hunting, a little of farming, much of fighting."

She sits at the table and gestures for me to retake my chair opposite her.

"Two chairs," I say, sitting. How had I not noticed?

"They stay with me a time, the Glysters. Often they are not in a good way. They are in need of fattening and strengthening. Sometimes just in need of kindness. Some have forgotten what kindness is and have to be reintroduced to the phenomena. One Glyster, Shorla, tried to kill me twice in my sleep because she couldn't conceive of a world where I wouldn't attempt to do the same thing to her." El grins. "Shorla Eemah. She could make it rain, even indoors. That was her Glyst. I think of her whenever it rains. I was thinking of her yesterday when I heard you splashing down the road like a drunken goat."

I remember my father saying, *Your aunty is horrible and loving, and she is also honest.* And I think, yes, she is horribly honest.

"If you stay with me, you will help me with my work," she says, seemingly oblivious to the insult she has just delivered. "I am responsible for a fifty-mile-wide strip, from here to the Forest of Leccan and the foothills of the Beorstehd Mountains. I travel out daily. Most days I go as far as I can and back again between sunrise and nightfall. Once a month, I travel to the mountains and back, a six-day round trip if I make good progress and there aren't too many… encounters."

"Why just that strip?" I ask. "Why just to the mountains?"

El smiles and winks at me.

"You're not as daft as you look, Alys."

"Thanks." I manage not to roll my eyes. El seems like someone who would not have much patience for such things.

"There are others," she says. "Others who cover the areas I do not. We call ourselves the Harbour. And the less you know about us for now, the better for us all."

"And what about the Dead City?" I ask.

El says nothing for a minute. Then, "I'll make some tea. I have some mamera leaves that should help with your ankle without dulling your wits too much further."

She says nothing while she makes the brew. She doesn't even look at me. It fills me with dread, her reluctance. I am close to telling her I do not wish to hear about the Dead City, that I will help her with her work and do not need to consider any other options, when she sets the cups of tea on the table, pushing mine toward me. It smells sweet and bitter at the same time. I remember that scent, from when I'd asked my mother about the Maddy Things and the Crawlies.

"The Dead City used to be called Utlath," El says. "In the old tongue, Utlath means indestructible or something similar." She snorts a laugh. "How could they not have known, the architects of that place, that bestowing such a name upon their own endeavour might invite the enmity of the gods? Utlath was the capital of the Glyst in our land of Abegan. There were other Glyst-gathering cities, in the world, beyond Abegan's shores—Edmod, Dryslic, Frofyr—but Utlath was by far the largest and finest. And it was the first to fall. There are few accounts of the actual order of events because few people survived the onslaught of the Cwalee. Some say the Maradyn assembled an army of Glysters, those who could throw fire from their hands or pull lightning from the sky or could smash castle walls with their fists. Some say this is nonsense because there was no time to assemble such an army, that Utlath fell in just a day. Whether it was a day or a month, whether there was a battle or just a massacre, it doesn't matter. The Cwalee fed and then they left. What remained was a dead city. *The* Dead City. A Glystless place."

El takes a sip of tea, and I do likewise.

"Of course," she continues, "there are many Glystless places. There have always been Glystless places, even during the Abundance. But Utlath had been *created* by the Glyst. And when the Glyst was gone from it, it was as a sheep's carcass after even the flies can find no more use for it. Some say the Maradyn were all killed by the Cwalee, that the Feeding was a fatal process. All that was left of a Cwalee victim, they say, was a withered thing, shrunk to the size of a child and quite dead. But that is not true. The Glysters I have met and helped have all been quite adamant about that. Some Maradyn survived the Feeding. They were small and withered, yes, but not dead. In fact, it seems these withered remnants of the Maradyn *cannot* die. They are called the Hollow. And they are always hungry. Not for food. They have passed beyond the need for physical sustenance. Their appetite is only for the Glyst. Some Glysters, who have grown tired of running and hiding, travel to the Dead City, to Utlath as was, and seek out the Hollow." Her face pinches in disgust. "They let the Hollow *feed* upon them until they are drained of every drop of the Glyst. Then they *try* to go back to their lives."

She sips her tea.

"Try," she says. "But it is never that simple. Those that have been drained are never the same. They spend their life longing for the Glyst, praying for it to return. But it does not, and theirs is a life of empty longing. They are, in their own way, no different from the Hollow."

"So, Alys, what's it going to be? The Work? Or the Dead City?"

Chapter 11

The Work

It is three months before El decides I am good enough to accompany her.

Up to that point, it is daily sword and bow practice. El is a better archer than my father and his equal with a sword. She teaches me unarmed combat techniques and how to use an opponent's size and strength against them. She teaches me which plants and berries to avoid and which can treat an infected wound or quench a fever. She has two horses—Skep and Rone—and she teaches me to ride the smaller of the two, Skep. I cannot ride well or fast, but I can ride relatively safely.

Whenever I blunder in my training or fail to follow her instructions to the letter, El snarls, "Were you raised by rocks, girl?" or "A welpa pup has more skill!" or, worst of all, "Are you sure you didn't die during the Ritual of the Seven Cuts and the Seven Cups? I am certain I am tutoring a corpse!"

When I do well in my training or surpass expectation, she just nods or, if she is feeling especially generous, says, "Not bad, not bad."

I am going through my sword drills when she appears with Skep and Rone. The horses are saddled and ready to ride.

Noticing my smile, she says, "Don't get too excited, Alys, we're just going to go a few miles out. We'll be back before dusk. The chances of us encountering a Glyster are very slim. I find three or four a year. One year, none. The most in a single year, seven."

We're at the edge of the nameless woodland on the opposite side of which is El's roundhouse when we hear the whistling of a grefa stone. I look across at El. She shakes her head, patting the pouch on her belt which contains her stone, wrapped in thick welpa leather.

"Not mine," she says, looking out across the copse-spotted grasslands that stretch out ahead of us toward the Forest of Leccan. It is a bright day, the sky blue-white, and I can make out the snow and ice that glitters on the peaks of the Beorstehd Mountains.

A figure emerges from a thicket of pale-yellow gelefed trees, a mile or so out. At this distance, I can't tell if it is a man, a woman or a child.

Without saying a word, El sets off toward the figure at a gallop.

Skep and I follow at a canter. I have set her to gallop only once, two weeks ago, and I found myself in a ditch with a goose egg on my forehead, no air in my lungs and El calling me a cwen, which is an old and very impolite word for a man who is so drunk he has soiled himself.

El reaches the figure in a minute. It is a boy, I see now, about my age. El dismounts, unshoulders her bow, nocks an arrow, training it on the thicket of gelefed trees. In the time it takes me to catch up, pulling Skep to an awkward staggering halt, three men emerge from the copse. I dismount with little or no grace and retrieve my own bow. As I am nocking an arrow, I glance across at the boy, and see it is a girl. Her hair is short and looks like it has been cut with a stone. There is more grime than skin visible on her face, and she is skinnier than the sickly gelefed trees behind her. I have never seen such fear on someone's face before.

"You cannot have him," says El.

The men look at each other and laugh. They are Leccans. Gafol would sometimes trade with the people of the forest, usually exchanging field grains for medicinal mushrooms and mosses, or the sweet sap of the red heafa trees. Clad in browns and greens, the Leccans before us are typically broad and tall, each bushy-bearded with long hair pulled up in a leather-bound knot. One carries a bow, another a two-handed battle axe, the last two smaller axes, one in each hand.

"He is ours," the bowman says over the whistle of the grefa stone, hanging from a cord around his neck. He has yet to nock an arrow, but his hand hovers above his quiver. "There is coin on his head. A lot of coin. Feeshun pays a pretty price for the blood of Glystgedders."

"Drop the bow and go back the way you came," says El.

"Don't be silly, woman," says the man with two axes, spinning the weapons. "This cannot end well for you. Jump back on your horse and trot off. You are no hunter, and we are not rabbits."

The Leccan with the battle axe laughs. But the bowman doesn't. Perhaps he has more sense than his companions. Perhaps it is that El's arrow is trained on him and one good bowman can recognise another, from their stance, steadiness and the look in their eye.

"Drop the bow and go back the way you came," says El.

"The boy is a danger to us all," says Two Axes. "Would you bring the Cwalee back to the world?"

"If you cared about that, the boy would be dead," says El, keeping her eye on the bowman. "Your talk of coin tells me you are a doubter in such matters."

Two Axes smirks.

"If you loose that arrow, my axe will find you the next second," he says.

"A coin says it doesn't," I say, training my own arrow on his chest.

Two Axes gives me the briefest of dismissive glances before looking back at El.

"You have a child for a bird dog," he sneers. "I doubt your qualities as a hunter. And as a marksman."

"Drop the bow and go back the way you came," says El. "I will do you the courtesy of giving you the count of three."

The axemen laugh. The bowman does not.

"*One*," says El.

And looses her arrow.

It strikes the bowman square in the throat, sinking in up to the fletchings. Blood, bright red on this bright day, jets from the wound. He drops his bow and attempts to clutch at the arrow's shaft, but his fingers scrabble at the empty air. He collapses, face down, his bulk muffling the grefa stone's whistling.

Two Axe's arm snaps back to launch his weapon, and I loose my arrow.

It strikes his shoulder with a satisfying *chuk* but he has already thrown his axe. It blurs toward El, but she is already stepping aside while nocking another arrow, and the axe passes her by.

Battle Axe is charging now, letting out a guttural roar. And Two Axes is preparing to throw his second missile. I nock an arrow, but I don't know which target El is going to choose. With no time to deliberate or confirm, I sink an arrow into Two Axe's chest. In almost the same moment, El's arrow lands an inch south of my own.

"Ged!" I hear her growl.

I turn to see her dropping her bow and drawing her sword.

Battle Axe sweeps at her in a wide arc and she manages, just, to step back from the blow. She jabs at him with her sword, but he is too distant. Already he is bringing the weapon back in a return arc. She dances back from the blade. It misses her by an inch.

I nock an arrow but El is between me and my target, a deliberate measure on Battle Axe's part I don't doubt. String half-pulled, I skip left until I have a clear shot. But Battle Axe sees me and moves to put El between us again.

"You will tire before me," he says through a gritted grin. "Both of you."

"I am already tired," says El and, letting her sword drop, she sits down cross-legged in front of the Leccan.

His feral grin evaporates.

My arrow finds his gut. It is not a fatal wound, but instinct causes him to drop his axe and attempt to staunch the wound.

El springs to her feet and puts her sword into his heart.

The Leccan falls first to his knees then, as El yanks her sword free of his chest, face down in the grass. She wipes the blood from her blade on the fallen man's back and turns back to face me.

"Get the boy," she says, pointing past me with her sword.

"The girl," I say, and look back to see she's fled a good hundred yards toward the road.

I catch up with her easily. She is tired, malnourished and smaller than me.

"Stop!" I shout after her. "We will not hurt you. We're here to help. The people who were after you are dead now."

The girl stops and turns to face me but continues backing away.

"And what do *you* want me for?" she demands.

"Nothing," I say. "We just want to help you."

"Why?"

"It's what we do. We're the Harbour. We help Glysters. I'm a Glyster, like you. I can bring the dead back to life. I saved my father."

"So? You're a Glyster. You think Glysters don't hurt other Glysters?"

"What's your Glyst?" I ask. "What's your gift?"

"Gift?" she sneers. "You call *this* a gift."

Her face begins to ripple. It is as if a breeze has got *under* her flesh. The ripples are slight to begin with but, within a few seconds, they are becoming increasingly pronounced and are accompanied by a sound I can only think of as fish-gutting. I hear hooves approaching behind me, but I can't bring myself to turn, to look away from the girl and her rippling flesh. But her flesh doesn't so much ripple now as undulate. It is stretching and lifting away from her skull. Her mouth, eyes and nostrils are just holes. I notice then that this undulating and lifting isn't limited to the girl's face. It's happening to her neck, her hands. And then the sheet that her flesh has become is *yanked* upwards above her head by some invisible hand. It hangs in the air, arms and legs billowing even though there is little wind in evidence. What it leaves behind is red and wet. Its eyes are wide and round, its teeth bared and white. It is a display of perfect butchery but clothed in ragged trousers and a tatty tunic.

The billowing flesh sheet swoops down and hovers in front of me at an arm's length. I stagger back two steps but somehow find the resolve to retreat no further. The slack mouth opens and, impossibly, a voice emerges, wispy but intelligible.

"You call this a gift?"

The red, wet figure falls to its knees and begins to weep, its head in its hands.

"If so," the sheet continues, "it is a cruel gift. And I do not want it."

From behind me, El says, "Then do not use it."

"Do you not think I would control it if I could? This... separation occurs when I am asleep, when I am frightened, if I laugh too much, if I cry. It happens when it will. I can *make* it happen, but I can't make it *not* happen."

"I can help you," says El. "I can take you to a Glyster who can help you control it."

"I don't want to control it. I don't want it at all. What good am I, save for frightening children on Wealdnight? I am looking for the Dead City, Utlath as was. There are things there, Glystleeches, that some call the Hollow. They will take this thing away from me. They will make me rid of it."

The skin sheet jerks up and away. As it does so, the weeping red thing stands. The sheet descends, then it *slithers* over its erstwhile frame, making wet, slapping sounds. In just a few seconds, it is as if frame and flesh had never been separated.

The girl turns and walks away.

"We can take you to the Dead City, if that is what you want," I say.

"Alys!" El snaps.

I turn and look at her.

"What?" I ask. "We can. Can't we?"

"We cannot," she says.

"But you said I could choose to go there if I wished. It was a choice between the Work and the Dead City. I chose the Work, but there *was* a choice."

"There was a choice," says El, handing me Skep's reins. "But I did not say I would take you." She climbs up onto Rone. "And I will not take the boy."

"Girl," I say.

"Does it matter whether I am a girl or a boy? I am skin and bone and all the stuff in between. That is all. I am Ethra Kell. And I do not need you to take me to the Dead City. I will find my own way."

"No," says El. "You will die long before you reach Utlath. You are hunted. Who is this Feeshun?"

"I don't know. I know only what you heard just now. That he pays money for Glyster blood."

"See?" says El, looking to me, then back to Ethra Kell. "There are dangers even I don't know of, and I know of many dangers to a Glyster such as yourself. How old are you?"

"It doesn't matter," she says.

"How old?"

"Thirteen," she says.

"Ethra," says El, her voice suddenly soft. "You will die."

"I would rather that," says Ethra. She slams the flat of her hand to her chest. "I would rather that than *this*."

"It is a gift," says El. "You might not know it yet, but it is a gift, this thing you can do."

"How can it be? How can the ability to *skin oneself* be a gift? It's a joke. The gods are making sport with me. I am the work of drunken Seros or Gewith in his foolish aspect. You will not change my mind."

Ethra turns and strides away.

El looks at me and shrugs. There is pain and sadness in her expression.

"The girl will die," she says.

"Not if we go with her. Not if we protect her."

"We cannot," says El. Then, "I will not."

"Will not?"

"I will not escort a Glyster to the Dead City and have this *blessing* sucked from them."

"But she will die. You said so. She is only thirteen!"

"Nevertheless, I will not help her. Not in that way. In every other way, yes. But not to squander the Glyst."

"And what if I had chosen to go to the Dead City? What then?"

"Then you would have gone alone, and all my prayers would have been with you."

I turn around and see that Ethra is almost at the tree line.

"Wait! Ethra! I am coming with you! I am coming with you to the Dead City."

"What?" says El. I hear her climb down from her horse and she grabs my shoulders. She tries to turn me to face her, but I keep my back to her.

Ethra has stopped now and is looking back at me.

"My mind is made up, El."

"No, Alys. You must rethink this. It is wrong. And it is too dangerous."

"It will be less dangerous for her if I am with her. The Freewood would have been dangerous for my father had I not been with him. He would be *dead* if I had not been with him. Not just because of my Glyst, but because I was his extra eyes and ears, a second blade. My mind is made up, El. It is made up and will not be changed."

Even as I hear the determination, the certainty, in my own voice, fear makes a nest in my belly, just as somewhere under the abandoned bridge on the edge of Gafol a straggis wasp has made a nest with the hair it pilfered from my scalp.

For the longest time, El doesn't speak. Then she says, "We will go back to my roundhouse—"

"No."

"We will go back to my roundhouse, you and Ethra and I—"

"No."

"We will go back to my roundhouse, you and Ethra and I, and we will prepare for your journey to the Dead City."

Chapter 12

The Road Widens

El moves our empty bowls and plates to the hearth and lays a map out on the table. It is a map of our land, of Abegan. It is shaped like a raindrop, Abegan, or like a dewdrop or a teardrop, depending on the poet or drunkard who is describing it at the time. To me, it has always been shaped as the swanstone pendant my mother used to wear. The swanstone is said to symbolise grace and strength in the face of adversity.

The map is old, brown and brittle, and El handles it with great care.

"This is the Dead City, Utlath as was." Her voice is flat, devoid of any enthusiasm.

She points to the coast at the bottom-right of the map, not quite where the droplet is fattest. Just beneath that, where it begins to thin again. The Dead City is represented by a drawing of three tall towers spiralling round one another like snakes in a nest. Off the coast, a little out to sea, is a drawing of a half-submerged creature that looks like a shark with the arms of a man.

"And here *we* are." El traces her finger back diagonally until it is high on the opposite side of the teardrop, not quite as far out to the coast as a picture of a headless fish that I assume represents Brim. "It will take you six days if you make good progress, only travelling by day. Do *not* go by night. Stick to the South Road for three days. Then, at Awlen," she taps a finger on a picture of a market tent near the middle of the map, "head east, along the Fisher Road. It will take you a further two days to get to Leax by the Eeffenn Sea. Follow the Coast Road south from Leax and you will arrive at the Dead City." She taps the intertwining towers again.

"Stick to the roads. Keep your ears tuned for the whistling of grefa stones. The South Road and the Fisher Road are both busy routes. And that's good. It's easier to be inconspicuous in crowds. Most people will be too busy trying to get to wherever they're going to take the least bit of interest in you. If anyone enquires as to your business, say you are going to Leax because you have heard there is work in the fish markets and you are good with a fleshing knife. It is a reasonable explanation, and mention of your skill with a blade may make those with dubious intentions think twice.

"I will give you enough supplies that you will not have to hunt or cook. If it gets cold at night, move around or keep close for warmth. Do not light a fire. Do nothing to draw attention to yourselves. Do not linger in any villages or towns along the way. People travelling ask few questions, but settlers are nosey and prone to gossip. You will need to memorise the aspects of the map pertinent to your journey. Spend an hour doing so, then get some sleep. You will need to leave at first light."

"Why can't we just take the map?" asks Ethra.

"Because it isn't mine to give. Besides, your journey is straightforward. At least from a directional point of view."

"And what about when we get to the Dead City?" I ask. "How do we find the Hollow?"

El shrugs. "I have no idea. I have only ever travelled as far as Leax. But I doubt you will have to look for the Hollow. I suspect the Hollow will find you."

I struggle to sleep that night. Not because of talk of the Hollow and the Dead City, even though both things trouble me. I struggle to sleep because I keep seeing the Leccans, Two Axes and Battle Axe, the life leaving them. They are the first men I have killed. And even though there had been no choice, it weighs on me more than I would have thought possible.

When, eventually, I do drift into sleep, I dream I am my father again. He is sitting on the foot of my bed in our roundhouse, holding the ragged blanket I could not be without when I was a toddler. He is thinking it is a good thing there has been a possible sighting of me west of the Forest of Leccan because that means his little Alys is still alive. But it also means Slek Mydra is one step closer to his prey. And Mydra's failure to find Alys these last three months has put him in a mood so foul his normally quiet voice has dropped to a little less than a whisper. It is said that Mydra speaks quietly so that to hear him speak, you are forced to move within his grasp.

I awaken to the sound of rain. It is not too heavy, not like the night Aunty Elsam found me, but it is unpleasant enough. It doesn't stop us, though. We are up, fed and astride Skep within the hour. The horse is strong enough to carry us both, but El recommends we give her a break every couple of hours. El has also clothed us against the rain, with hooded cloaks that have been treated with waterproofing oils.

"I will not try to change your mind," says El. "But if you change it yourself, there is no shame in that. And when you are done, you are welcome back here. Even Glystless."

"Thank you, El," I say. "Please do not think my decision reflects badly on you."

Her eyes widen.

"It reflects badly on the composition of your brain, child," she says. She turns and walks back into her roundhouse and closes the door.

"What are you waiting for?" says Ethra. "Let's go."

I do not know. I do not know what I am waiting for. But for a good few seconds, I am unable to do anything but sit there, staring out at the road ahead and the rain. Then I give Skep a light squeeze with my calves and she begins to walk.

The rain stops after about an hour and we take down our hoods. We make good progress, even though the road—largely disused since the Abundance—is poor. I smile when I think that if I'd travelled this road in the opposite direction, I would likely be back at the bridge now with its straggis wasp nests and Eftas Hilder's arrows still spiking the soil near where I hid in the red caitlins.

That seems such a long time ago now. And yet so very recent. Time is like the ground, the old saying goes: unnoticed till we fall.

"Where are you from?" I ask Ethra.

"Mella," she replies. "Between the Forest of Leccan and the mountains."

I've heard of it, I think.

"Where the apples come from?" I ask.

"The orchards are what the town's known for, I suppose. The smell of apples makes me sick if I'm being honest. I prefer a big strawberry. Or yellowberries."

The mention of yellowberries makes me think of Dwynan Furral, of the time we kissed, and of the time I last saw him, being chased by a near-dead scabwolf. I am certain he must have got away. I hope so. He might not have spoken to me after we kissed, but that hardly warrants the death penalty.

We spend the next hour, Ethra and I, talking about favourite foods, and then the rough road we are riding along merges with the wide South Road.

I have never seen a road so big. Fifteen horses could ride abreast on it with ease.

Before the sun begins to set, we pass several people heading north and are overtaken by several heading south at a brisker pace than us. As El had given us to expect, none of them show the least interest in us.

Before the sun sinks below the horizon, I take Skep off the road, down a short slope and into a copse of trees.

"We'll stay here for the night," I tell Ethra, climbing down from the horse then helping her do likewise. We lay out our bedrolls and place sprigs of drifan at the four corners of our camp, to repel biting and stinging insects. The food El gave us is largely flavourless—dried meat and fish, pipnuts and berries—but we are both hungrier than we would have thought possible after an uneventful day of sitting.

Ethra yawns and lies back on her bedroll, pulling her cloak over her as a blanket. I do the same, suddenly exhausted.

Ethra points up at the sky.

"Look," she says. "There is Fryth, God of Peace."

I just see stars. Thousands of them. Some like candlebugs, others like a faintly luminous dust.

"And there, right next to Fryth," she continues, "is Guth, God of War. Some say they are one and the same. They say Fryth is simply Guth exhausted from battle, and Guth is Fryth driven mad by inactivity and boredom." She points again. "And there is—" She sits bolt upright, eyes wide with fear. "Do you hear that?" she whispers.

I sit up and shake my head.

"I hear nothing."

"There," she says.

I shake my head again.

"What?" I ask.

"Whistling," she says.

And then I hear it—faint or distant—the whistling of a grefa stone.

Chapter 13

A Coin on My Head

I hear the words of my Aunty Elsam.

You have two options when you hear the whistling of a grefa stone. Move away from it quickly until you are out of its sight. Or go to it and seize it by any means necessary. Flee it, or silence it. No other choices.

But El also told us not to travel by night. So fleeing is not an option.

Which leaves going to the source of the sound and silencing it.

I get out from under my blanket and grab my sword.

"Stay here," I say to Ethra.

I turn slowly on the spot, trying to get a sense of the direction from which the whistling is coming. North, I think. Back the way we came.

A chill grips my spine and pulls my skin tight to my bones.

Could it be Slek Mydra? My stomach turns at the thought, and I swallow so hard my throat clicks like snapped fingers.

My stomach turns again when I realise the whistling is getting closer. The urge to decamp and move in the opposite direction as fast as we can is so tempting I almost relent. But if we flee by road, we will be out in the open and exposed. If we travel off-road, in the dark, we will likely get lost or hurt.

A third option presents itself. I do not have to go to the source of the whistling. I could wait for it to come to me. I could set an ambush. I sheath my sword, grab my bow and quiver and head up the slope to the roadside. I find a clump of caitlins, flowerless this time of year, but still leafy at the stem. Kneeling, I nock an arrow and wait. I can see perhaps a hundred yards before the road melts into blackness.

The whistling is getting louder, closer, but only by slow degrees. A cramp begins to prod at my left thigh and there is an ache in my lower back that is almost a burning.

And then I can't tell if the whistling *is* getting closer.

I listen for a full minute, turning all my attention to the sound of the grefa stone, trying to block out all other sounds—insects, night birds and, somewhere, the shrill bark of a fox.

The whistling is steady. The stone is no longer on the move. I am certain.

Have I been seen? Is someone with better eyesight than I standing just beyond the range of my own vision, there where the road pinches into darkness? And what if he has a longbow, this nighthawk? I am well within range of such a weapon. I might, if I am very alert, hear the snap of the bowstring the instant before the arrow finds its mark.

I try to *will* myself smaller, less visible.

And suddenly I am furious at myself.

Three months ago, I was hiding in a cluster of caitlins, willing myself smaller, shrinking from the inexpert arrows of the idiot Hilder brothers. Am I no better now than I was then? Have all the aches and pains and harsh blows with the flat of Aunty Elsam's blade been for nothing?

The grefa stone continues to issue its unfaltering whistle.

Seize it by any means necessary, I hear Aunty Elsam say. And I see her in my mind's eye, nodding with very slight approval. *Not bad. Not bad.*

I ease myself out of my hiding placing and head back down the slope. But instead of heading back to the camp and Ethra, I make my way north alongside the road, weaving through saplings and clusters of caitlins. After about fifty yards, I head back up to the road in a half-crouch, emerging by another bunch of caitlins.

I listen. The whistling is closer now. I listen for a minute more. The stone is still motionless. I stare into what looks like the same patch of darkness I'd scrutinised fifty yards back.

I scuttle back down the slope and progress another fifty yards, then head back up to the road. Still no sign of the stone's owner. But the whistling is so loud now he *must* be in sight. The stone cannot be more than ten yards away at that volume. A brief panic seizes me, and I have to stop myself from randomly loosing arrows into the darkness ahead of me in the hope that one or two might find their target.

Then I see it.

The grefa stone.

In the middle of the road. Just lying there as if dropped, like a lost object.

Only while it would be possible to lose a silent grefa stone—as it would be to lose any stone—it would not be possible, surely, to lose a whistling grefa stone.

Too late, I hear footfalls behind me, approaching fast. I know from my training with El that every instinct will tell me to turn and face the threat, to shield myself from whatever blow might fall.

But that is not the way it is done, I hear her say.

I drop to my right, loose as if in a swoon, and I hear a weapon cutting the air where I was crouching just a moment ago. Still loose—*like a chatta puppet with its strings cut*, El says—I let myself flop down the slope, away from the road. I lose my bow, but when I reach level ground, I spring up and draw my sword.

My attacker is already striding toward me.

He is not Slek Mydra.

He looks to be about my age, maybe a year or two older. He has the black hair of the Scur, those people who dwell at the far northern tip of Abegan. But they are supposed to be a sturdy folk, and this boy is lean, his face a little drawn.

As he approaches, he draws his sword. In his other hand is a leather sap. So, he wasn't trying to kill me, just render me unconscious.

"Look," he says. "I don't want to hurt you." There is a lilt to his voice that confirms he is of Scur blood despite his build.

I say nothing.

Do not indulge in fighting talk, I hear El say. *It is a waste of breath and you will tire sooner. Let your opponent talk all they want.*

"Put the sword down, girl. You'll hurt yourself."

He lunges forward and jabs the tip of his blade at me. I knock it away easily with my own. And he swipes with the sap. He is tall—half a foot taller than me—and his reach is long. I feel the wind from the sap as it passes an inch from my nose.

When it has passed, I jab with my own blade. He skips back and swings the sap again, a wide arc. I meet it with my sword, splitting the leather. Stones spill from it, scattering about the ground, a few bouncing from my legs.

He drops what is now a useless scrap of leather and swaps his sword from his left to his right hand. I take advantage of the manoeuvre to swing at him. He manages—just—to parry. I press, giving him no opportunity to counterattack.

He is a reasonable swordsman. He parries using the minimum effort possible. He is waiting for me to tire, to slow. He keeps moving back, forcing me to stretch, to use more energy. If we go on like this, I will give him the opening he is looking for. I need to finish him quickly. I slash at him and when he parries, I jab hard. The tip of my sword strikes his gut, but a backward leap and his leather tunic prevent any penetration. I hear him grunt, though, as some of the wind goes out of him.

He swipes at me, but it is a move borne of panic or anger, and I knock it aside with ease. My counterattack strikes the shoulder of his right arm. It cuts him deep enough that the arm weakens and he almost loses his sword. He attempts to pass it back to his left hand, but I catch the weapon in flight, knocking it to the ground.

He steps back, hands raised in surrender.

"Okay, okay," he says, catching his breath. "I yield. The coin on your head is not worth a gutting."

"What coin?"

"The Jarl of Gafol has placed a bounty on your head," he says. "Shame, I have to say. It's a very nice head."

"Who is it you think I am?"

"Alys Clainh. Daughter and son of Aryc Clainh. Alys Clainh, who endured the Ritual of the Seven Cuts and the Seven Cups. Alys Clainh, Glyster." He lowers his hands. "But none of that matters to me. I'll be on my way. It will be as if we never met."

"I can't allow that."

"Look. No harm done. Well…" He glances at his shoulder. I can see fresh blood. It gleams wetly in the moonlight. "I'll just be on my way. Penniless, but alive. As always."

"I can't allow that. If the Jarl finds out my father lied, he will…"

I will cut off your hands and put out your eyes and send you down to the Woever where the scabwolves skulk.

"Look," says the Scur. "I'll tell the Jarl I approached you, but the grefa stone was silent. Then I'll say you got away. This is just about the coin to me. I'll find another way to earn it."

"I cannot trust a man who would creep up behind someone with a sap in hand."

I step toward him, sword raised. He reaches for a dagger sheathed on his belt, but I know he will not have the opportunity to use it.

And then I see the Leccans, Two Axes and Battle Axe, the look on their faces as the life bled from them. Bled from them through the wounds I had inflicted. And then it is the Ritual of the Seven Cuts and the Seven Cups once more, and the Jarl is dragging the whetted flint from my hairline to the nape of my neck. I feel light-headed. The periphery of my vision darkens. My sword feels heavy in my hands. It droops.

I see the hilt of the Scur's dagger come at me through the growing darkness. It is a pretty thing, white bone, carved in the shape of one of the Sea Ladies that are said to swim off the coast at Leax, with tail and scales where legs should be.

And then I see nothing, and the whistling of the Scur's grefa stone out on the road pursues me into unconsciousness.

Chapter 14

Casmel Durn

It seems like my eyes are shut for only a moment, for a little more than a blink. But that can't be right because my hands and feet are bound, and the Scur is sitting opposite me on a blanket, tending his wound. The wound I gave him.

Mine is not his only wound. He has removed his tunic and shirt and I can count ten scars from where I am lying in the dirt. He catches me looking and grins.

"Don't covet what you can't afford, lass," he says. "I see you admiring my battle scars and more besides."

Embarrassment turns to anger as I see my bow, quiver and sword at his feet.

"That is my father's sword," I say. "Lift it from the dirt."

"It's just metal," he says. "Just metal sharpened to a blade and a point. It's just a tool."

But he picks it up and puts it on the blanket next to him.

"For what it's worth, I am sorry," he says. "But coin is coin. And my… I am in need of it. You would do the same in my place."

"The Jarl will kill me. And he will kill my father."

The Scur busies himself putting on his shirt and tunic. He does not meet my eye. Then he goes to his horse and makes an unnecessary task of adjusting the nosebag from which it is eating. It is a poor man's horse, small and plain, but it looks well cared for.

"As I say, I am sorry for it." He still refuses to look at me. "But if I do not bring you in, Slek Mydra will. At least I will take you in alive. You could plead for clemency for your father."

"You have ged for thoughts if you believe such a thing. You're an idiot as well as a coward."

"Coward?" He turns now and not only looks at me, but glares at me. "Think of the risk I'm taking keeping you alive. You are as a beacon fire to the Cwalee. If I were a coward, I'd gut you where you lay."

"Perhaps you lack the stomach for butchery," I say. "Perhaps you are squeamish."

"Squeamish?" He slides his dagger from his belt and walks toward me. "Would you have me gut you? Would you have me open you up from collar to girdle? I have no fear of a little blood and gristle."

But his face is suddenly a rigid mask of fear.

He is staring past me. I twist and turn so I am facing the way he is looking.

Ethra Kell is standing at the edge of the clearing where the Scur has made camp. At least part of her is. The glistening, red part. Her skin is nowhere to be seen. She is aiming an arrow at the Scur's chest. She appears to be grinning, but that is probably due to the absence of lips.

"In the name of Memynd," the Scur mutters. "In the name of Memynd, God of Madness."

Then, out of the darkness just beyond Ethra's fleshless form, her skin appears, gliding, billowing. One arm is held out, the empty glove of a hand wrapped about a knife.

"Drop the blade," says Ethra's undulating skin, in that wispy, wind-through-a-keyhole voice.

"Dro' the lade," says the skin's lipless counterpart.

I hear the dagger strike the ground with a gritty thud behind me.

"In the name of Memynd," the Scur mutters again, so little strength in his voice he sounds on the verge of fainting.

"Now turn about and kneel," says Ethra's skin. "And put your hands on top of your head."

"Turn a'out and kneel," says Ethra's body. "And 'ut your hands on your head."

I hear scuffling as the Scur follows Ethra's instructions. *Both* Ethras' instructions.

Ethra's skin glides toward me and settles on the ground at my side, her legs like discarded trousers. She puts the knife to work on the Scur's bonds and, in a few seconds, I am free. I rub my wrists and ankles, even though I had not been bound so tight as to leave a mark. It is more the memory of the bonds I am trying to erase. It reminds me too much of the Ritual, of hanging like a foorstig. I stand and pain fills my head.

"You've got quite the bump on your noggin," says Ethra's skin, and she brushes her fingertips over a tender spot above my left temple.

"Shall I kill hin'?" says Ethra's body.

I look at the Scur kneeling in the dirt with his hands on his head.

"Yes," says Ethra's skin. "We must. If we don't, he will only follow us. Or tell others of our whereabouts."

But putting an arrow in a charging Leccan is one thing; an execution is another. My own words mock me from the very recent past: *Perhaps you lack the stomach for butchery. Perhaps you are squeamish.*

"Yes," says Ethra's body. "We will 'e dead long 'efore we reach the Dead City if we let hi' live."

"The Dead City?" says the Scur. "You are travelling to Utlath?"

I glare at Ethra's body.

"Why would you tell him that, loose lips?" I say.

"I don't ha' any li's," she replies, and Ethra's skin gives a breathy laugh at that.

"I'll come with you," says the Scur, words emerging in a desperate rush. "I told you this was just about the coin. I can get a fair coin for grefa stones, and the Dead City is full of them. I would never have chanced such a task alone, but three of us—"

"Grefa stones?" I say.

"Yes, they're made from pieces of the Dead City. Pieces of the walls and buildings. It is said the very structure of Utlath cries out for the Glyst. Grefa stones are just chunks of Utlath with a hole poked through. Did you not know? And people pay heavy coin for them. *Heavy* coin. If I get enough of them, I will earn three or four times the bounty placed on your head."

"We can't trust him," says Ethra's skin.

"I shall 'ut an arrow in his 'ack," says Ethra's body with a tone of finality.

"No," I say. "Three of us will stand a better chance than two in our bid to get to the Dead City."

I surprise myself at how sincere I sound, because I know the real reason I want to take him up on his offer is that I have no stomach for an execution. I am squeamish.

"I think that is a bad idea," says Ethra's skin.

"A 'ery, 'ery, 'ad idea," says Ethra's body.

"We will take his weapons and bind his hands," I say. "You will ride behind him on his horse. If he does anything—*anything*—foolish, it will be the last foolish things he does." I turn to him. "Will your horse be any trouble?"

"Lata? No. No trouble. She is sweet and daft. And I'm Casmel, Casmel Durn. My friends call me Cass."

"We have no need of your name," I say.

"And we are not your friends," says Ethra's skin.

I collect my weapons and lead his horse back to our camp. Ethra, all of a piece now, takes his travelling bag, sword and dagger. He was speaking true of Lata. She is no trouble.

Once the Scur is bound and propped against a tree stump, I go through his bag.

"That's private," he says, wincing as he strains at his bonds. I have not been as considerate as he.

The bag contains everything I would have expected. Dried meat, nuts and berries; a small pouch of medicinal herbs; some fishing tackle; a flint stone and tinder; a few coins; a stone cup; and, bundled tight in leather and wool, the grefa stone. It begins whistling the moment I start to unwrap it.

I touch it, but it refuses to be silenced.

Ethra, I realise.

I hold it out to her.

"Touch it," I say.

"I would rather not," she says.

"It is the only way to silence the wretched thing."

It takes her a minute to find the courage, but then she taps it lightly with the very tip of her finger, as one might test a heated pot. Her skin ripples with repulsion. But the stone, at last, falls silent.

I wrap the stone, return it to the bag and continue my search. There is a set of spedig tiles—thin slices of whalebone with various gods depicted on them—a tatty strip of leather with a knot at one end, and sketched onto a thin sheet of whitebark, a reasonable likeness of me.

Scowling, I push the whitebark back into the bag. I wonder how many of those likenesses have been passed about and how far south they've travelled.

"What's this?" I ask, holding up the strip of leather.

His face darkens,

"Nothing," he says. "Put it back. Please."

"What are you planning to do with all this 'coin' you're always going on about?" asks Ethra.

"My father has gambling debts," he says. "He stands to lose everything."

I put the leather strip back in the bag and take out the pouch of spedig tiles.

"Is this how he accumulated his debt?" I ask. "Spedig?"

"Yes. I tried to win it back for him," he says. "I've played in tournaments all over Abegan. But everything I win, I lose. I have never been in debt, at least not much, but nor have I been in credit for very long."

"It is a fool's game, spedig," I say.

"Aye," he says with a weariness that does not sit right with someone of his age. "Some say Gewith, God of Luck, created the game. But Gewith is also the God of Folly."

"My father says Gewith must have been drinking with Seros when he designed the game," I say.

"Your father sounds wise," he replies. "Wiser than mine. But that's not a difficult thing."

Ethra and I take it in turns to sleep, so that one of us is always watching the Scur.

It is light when I awaken. Ethra is sound asleep, her mouth hanging open.

And the Scur is gone.

Chapter 15

A Plan of Sorts

"Ged! Ethra! He's gone." I jump to my feet and grab my sword.

Ethra sits up, eyes wide. For a moment, her skin begins to ripple, but then it settles.

"What?" she says.

"The Scur. He's gone."

"Said you should have let me put an arrow in his back," she says, voice sleep-slurred. "But you didn't listen."

Then I notice his bag is still where I left it, next to my bedroll. What's more, Lata is still tied to a nearby tree. Why would the Scur leave them behind?

"I will not be bound," he says from behind me.

I pivot on one heel, slashing with my sword, but he's a good three yards away and I look foolish.

He is unarmed, his hands filled with bright-red water apples.

"There is a stream about half a mile from here," he says. "Lots of these little beauties."

I track him with the tip of my sword as he walks back into the camp.

"I could have run," he says. "I could have taken Lata and been away. But I was speaking the truth about going with you to Utlath. There is more coin to be made there than from trading in your pretty head." He lets the water apples fall onto my blanket, keeping one, which he feeds to Lata. "Help yourselves. They're delicious."

Ethra doesn't need to be asked twice. She grabs an apple and consumes more than half in a single bite. Pink juice runs down her chin. Her eyes roll back, and she lets out a groan of delight.

I sheath my sword and, affecting an air of only half-interest, pick up an apple, shine it on my sleeve and take a bite.

"Not bad," I say, reminding myself of El at her most effusive. It is the first time I have had a water apple, and it is divine. Sweet, juicy, fragrant and with a little saltiness that lifts all the other flavours. "Not bad at all." I finish it and help myself to another.

"So, Alys," says the Scur. "What's the plan?"

"Well… Master Durn," I say.

"Cass."

I sigh. "Well, Casmel, we cannot go by road now. Not now there are pictures of me in circulation. We'll just have to follow the road as best we can from a safe distance."

"That will be slow going," says Ethra. "It will add a week to our journey. We don't have enough supplies to last that long."

"We could go wide of the South Road," says Casmel. "Head south-east and meet the Fisher Road halfway along. That should put us back on schedule."

"Have you been that far from the Roads before?" I ask.

He produces a grim smile. "No. I've always travelled by the Roads."

"So, you've no idea what we might encounter?"

Another grim smile, almost a wince. "No idea whatsoever."

"So, we stay parallel to the South Road, then the Fisher Road," I say. "We stick to the plan. We'll just have to reduce our ration intake. And we could find food along the way. Like these water apples."

"It's possible," says Casmel. "But what if there is no food to be found."

"I can catch game," I say.

"But that means a fire," says Ethra. "El said no fires."

"It's the least risky option," I say. "We can keep the smoke to a minimum and put it out once the food is cooked."

"There is another option," says Casmel. He goes to his bag, rummages for a moment and comes out with a small pouch. At first, I think it's his medicine bag. But then he gives it a shake and it rattles. The spedig tiles. "We're two days from Awlen. There's always a spedig game happening somewhere. You two can wait for me just outside the town. I make some coin, pick up some supplies then meet you back at the camp."

"Doesn't sound completely stupid," says Ethra.

"I don't know," I say. "How do we know you won't make your money and go, then make some more money telling the Jarl or Slek Mydra where we might be found?"

"I'll leave Lata with you. I've known her since she was a foal."

"I still don't think—"

"I can't possibly make as much money at spedig as I can from collecting and selling grefa stones."

Eventually, I say, "Very well. But we need to get moving now. Using the South Road, it would take two days to get to Awlen. Now, off-road, it's going to be three. More if we don't keep moving."

We're decamped and riding in less than fifteen minutes, Ethra sitting behind Casmel, her arms round his waist. For the time being, we're able to ride parallel, and Casmel looks across at me and says, "I know Ethra's Glyst well enough, but what's yours?"

"I can bring the dead back to life. I'm not sure how it works. A slite mortally wounded my father.

I… I sort of pulled the life from the slite and put it in my father."

"And he was… normal? When he came back?"

"I… think so. I don't know."

For the first time, I wonder. What does it mean to have cheated death? What consequences might there be?

Casmel looks over his shoulder at Ethra. "Does it hurt? When your skin… comes off? Is it painful?"

"Not really. I feel kind of numb when it happens. It's very disorientating. It's like there are two of me and one of me at the same time. Mostly it's like I take it in turns. One moment I'm the body-me, the next I'm the skin-me. But sometimes I am both. Seeing two sights at once. It's nauseating."

"You'd make a great thief," says Casmel. "You could slide your skin under a door then let your body in."

"I do not want to be a thief. I want to be normal."

"Is that why you're going to the Dead City? To seek the Hollow?"

"You know about that?" says Ethra.

"Yes. Spedig is played at night, usually where there is drink. People who drink talk a lot and their attention always wanders toward the strange."

The track we are following narrows as woodland surrounds us and, for the next three hours, we ride single file and there is no conversation. I prefer it that way. Casmel strikes me as one of those people who is afraid that an unchecked silence can grow and become something insurmountable. There is an old Northern saying: When the tongue flaps too much, thoughts are blown away.

As if he has registered my preference for silence and wishes to irritate me, Casmel starts up jabbering again. He is talking to Ethra, so I can't hear everything he's saying. The only sentence I catch in full is when he asks Ethra if the skin-her has ever got stuck in a tree on a windy day, like a kite. Ethra's response is short and brutal. Casmel begins to defend himself but stops mid-sentence, perhaps thinking better of it.

Then I see the arrow protruding from his neck. The side of his face is glossed red with blood.

Chapter 16

Ambush

Casmel's hand goes to the arrow, and he falls from Lata, taking Ethra with him.

The arrow came from the left, and I look in that direction. The upward-sloping woodland is dense, but I think I see a movement no more than twenty or thirty yards away, up on the bough of a vine-strangled oak. Someone dressed in dull greens and browns, their face mud-caked.

An arrow misses me by such a slim margin, I feel its fletchings brush my forehead.

I jump down from Skep, slapping her rump hard so she runs on to safety. Lata, not so daft as Casmel would have us believe, follows. I look for cover and see a tree stump sprouting green ferns and orange mushrooms in equal number. Scrambling, I put it between myself and our ambusher. The moment I am out of sight, I hear an arrow strike the stump's rotted wood. There is a stink like spoilt meat as the arrow doubtless demolishes a cluster of mushrooms.

I unshoulder my bow and nock an arrow.

I hear Casmel moaning and gurgling and, off to my right, a thrashing of undergrowth. I glance across and see Ethra pushing herself back against a tree, her arms pulled in tight.

"How many?" she says.

"One?" I say, shrugging. I'm hoping it's just one, a lone bandit. But who knows?

Ethra holds up three fingers and points to herself, then holds up four and points to me.

I nod, draw my bow and prepare to stand.

Ethra counts to three on her fingers, then bobs her head out from behind the tree and then pulls it back again.

On four, I stand.

An arrow strikes Ethra's tree with a thud.

I don't have time to seek a target. I just let my arrow fly where I last saw movement, up in the vine-choked oak. Before I drop back behind the stump, I am rewarded with a cry of shock and pain. A moment later, an arrow passes overhead and buries itself in a tree behind me. If I'd remained standing for a second more, the arrow would have struck me square in the chest.

A second ambusher.

Lucky, I think. Lucky, Alys. But luck is a bucket with a hole. I wonder how much luck is left in mine?

There is a longer version of the saying about luck and buckets.

Luck is a bucket with a hole, but a capable hand can plug it for a time.

I look at the arrow that was meant for me. It is protruding from the tree at an angle, its fletchings pointing a little to the right. In my mind, I draw a line. As long as he stays put, I'll have a chance.

"There are two of them, then?" says Ethra.

I nod.

"There are three of us," says Ethra.

"Casmel has an arrow in him," I say. "Did you not see? He will not live."

"I saw. I have his blood on me. But I'm not talking about Cass."

"What?" I say. Then, "Oh."

Already Ethra's flesh is beginning to ripple as it did just two days ago—just *two days* ago?—after our confrontation with the Leccan. It ripples, then it undulates, then it whips up and away, going up high into the tree above her.

I nock an arrow.

"Up here, you gedsacks!" says Ethra, her voice loud despite its wispiness. "Here I am! Trapped like a kite on a windy day!"

I hear not one, but two arrows strike wood.

I stand, turn in the direction of the line I drew in my mind and loose my arrow.

Luck is a bucket with a hole, but a capable hand can plug it for a time.

Before I take cover, I hear my arrow strike something both hard and soft. I know that sound: flesh and bone. Once I am back behind the stump, I hear a drawn-out growl of agony that ceases abruptly. Please, let him be dead. Please, let him be in the grip of Wealm. Let the God of Death have him in his grasp.

From up-slope, I hear a thud and the thrashing of ferns. The ambusher who was in the vine-choked tree—wounded but not mortally so—has dropped from his perch and is making his bid for escape. I see it in my mind's eye.

A part of me thinks to let him go. What danger is he now? Doubtless wounded and afraid? Let him go. Let him flee.

Another part, a *new* part, knows that he has seen us, that it is a risk too far to let him go. That he holds in his hand my father's life.

I stand, nocking an arrow.

I see him running up the slope. He is making slow progress, one hand pressed to his thigh. He either injured himself when he dropped from the bough, or that's where my arrow caught him. Even limping, he will be out of range of my arrow in a few seconds.

I draw back the bowstring, take careful aim and loose my arrow.

It strikes him in the middle of his back. I hear the crunch even from this distance. The crunch of arrowhead against spine. His legs cease to work, and he drops to the ground and begins tumbling down the slope. He is screaming when his descent begins, silent when he reaches the track at the bottom, a tangle of limbs and wide, white eyes staring out of a grimy face, jaw hanging slack and wide.

I look down the track. Lata has returned and is nosing at Casmel's motionless form.

From behind me, Ethra says, "Can you bring him back?"

I turn. She has reassembled herself, but her skin is still settling, pulling tight here and there.

"I don't know," I say, making my way toward Casmel. "With my father, it just happened. I don't know how to make it happen."

Casmel is lying on his back, one hand still loosely closed about the shaft of the arrow that killed him. He has the same look in his eye as his murderer. And that seems unfair, that ambusher and ambushed should look the same in death.

I've been a fool. If I'd stayed with El, this wouldn't have happened. We should have tried harder to make Ethra stay. We should have chased any notions of going to the Dead City and seeking the Hollow from her silly little head. We should have tied her to a post until she came to her senses. Surely she would have done so sooner or later?

I remember El saying to Ethra, *I can help you. I can take you to a Glyster who can help you control it.* If I'd stayed with her, El would doubtless have taken me to someone who could have taught me how to control my Glyst, and I wouldn't be staring down dumbly at Casmel Durn's lifeless face. I would know what to do.

I'm such a gedding *fool*.

An ember of anger ignites in my belly. And I remember.

"I was angry," I say, turning to Ethra. "I was angry when I did it last time. When I brought my father back."

"Angry?" says Ethra.

"Yes, I—"

Ethra slaps me so hard across the face, I taste blood.

"Are you angry now?" she asks, grinning.

Before I can reply, she slaps me again.

The ember ignites. I feel its heat rise into my chest, my neck, my face. It surges down my arms to the tips of my fingers.

I turn back to Casmel, kneel next to him. I move his still-warm hand away from the arrow, then grab the shaft. I grit my teeth, look away and pull. I feel the barb snag. I pull harder. I hear the tearing of flesh. I look back at Casmel. The wound is unreasonably large, and ragged. Fresh blood spills from it. I drop the arrow and put both my hands to the wound.

There is a hiss. A thick ribbon of steam rises from the wound.

Casmel's eyes flicker behind his eyelids.

And then I am nowhere. I am Nowhere.

I am in the same blackness in which I found myself after I put my hand to my father's wound. I try to lift my hands before my eyes and, just as last time, I have no hands to see, no eyes with which to see them. I am bodiless and calm. As before, I have an almost overwhelming desire to stay in this Nowhere, in this place of troublelessness.

And then there is a ripple.

The stone has hit the lake.

And I hear the voice of my mother. Or I imagine I do.

It is about the Big Things. The Gods.

And I am back in the woods off the South Road, kneeling next to Casmel. I am there with such an abruptness that I jerk like someone half asleep prodded with a sharp stick.

I lift my right hand from Casmel's wound. Steam still hangs in the air before me. I turn and point a bloody finger past Ethra at the tangled form of the ambusher. Keeping my finger trained on the bandit's corpse, I turn back to Casmel and press my left hand harder against the wound, fingers splayed. I stop breathing. I do not hold my breath. I just stop breathing.

"It is coming," says a low, fractured voice behind me.

I turn and look up at Ethra. She is looking at me, at my hand on Casmel's wound. She does not appear to have heard the voice.

"It is coming." It is the corpse that speaks, though its wide-hanging mouth doesn't move. "The Gravene."

The bandit's forehead ripples, like Ethra's when her skin is about to come loose, and then an apple-sized ball of pale pink light rises out of the ripples. The light bobs toward me, and the corpse from which it rose collapses in on itself, as if a whole clew of rotworms have fed on its offal in an instant.

An inch from my bloody fingertip, the ball of light stops. Again that smell: blackberries and rose petals.

I stretch my arm a little and touch the light.

And then I am looking up at the canopy.

Ethra's face appears, then Casmel's, caked in dried blood on the left side, from jaw to temple.

"I was dead," he whispers. With the heel of his hand, he wipes tears from his eyes. "I was dead."

"Did you ride an Unrim?" asks Ethra, excited. "Did you ride an Unrim to the River of Honey?"

"There were no Unrim," he says. "And there was no River of Honey. It was just like here." He waves an arm about. "Except there was no colour, because everything was covered in tiny grey mushrooms. Even me. And there was no sound. And the woods were filled with skinny people-things, made of smoke except wet and sticky. There were lots of them. They had holes where faces should have been, and I could feel them watching me even though they had no eyes." He shivers like a frozen child. "I never want to see that place again."

Chapter 17

Foreg, God of Deceits and Disguises

We reach the outskirts of Awlen in three days, late in the afternoon. We encounter no more bandits en route, and although we see signs of a variety of dangerous creatures—claw marks on trees, nef droppings and the large three-toed print of an ashex—nothing troubles us. Only the terrain slows us down: dense woodland, mud, brambles or a combination of all three.

We do not speak at all on the first day. Even Casmel. Especially Casmel. On the second day, conversation recommences, but we only speak of trivial things. Nobody mentions the attack, Casmel's death or subsequent resurrection. But as we see the steeply sloping slate rooftops of Awlen rising over the horizon, Ethra turns to Casmel and says, "Did it hurt? The arrow in your neck."

He grins, "It was like being stung by a wasp. A wasp the size of a carthorse."

"There's no mark," says Ethra. "Not even a little scar. I sat on a boning knife when I was ten and there's still a fine scar on my bum."

I laugh. "We do not need to hear about the distinguishing details of your bum, Ethra."

"I was just making a point," she says.

"No," says Casmel. "I think it was the boning knife that made the point." And he gives a little nod and a wink, as my father does whenever he says something he mistakenly believes is amusing.

We make camp in a small copse and, as we eat, Casmel attempts to teach us the basics of spedig. It is lost on me. The tiles each depict one of the gods. Some gods are of more value than others, some gods can form alliances with gods in the same hand and some have enmity toward one another and devalue the hand. The best hand, as far as I can make out, is one in which there is a three-way alliance and at least one god that shows enmity toward a god in an opposing player's hand. Fryth, the God of Peace, and Foreg, the God of Deceits and Disguises, are the most important tiles. Fryth can quench the enmity of other gods, and Foreg can become any tile that is not already in the player's hand. It strikes me as sad that the most coveted tile in a game of spedig is the most duplicitous.

Casmel makes sure Lata is well fed, shoulders his bag—containing only his tiles, coin and that strange strip of knotted leather—and says, "Right. Wish me luck!"

"May Gewith be with you," says Ethra.

"And Foreg," I suppose.

"If both are with me, the pot is mine." He puts a hand to his neck, where the arrow struck him. "Although I may have already spent any coin with the face of Gewith stamped upon it."

"Let's hope not," I say.

"I will see you at first light, with supplies and a mild hangover."

"Do not drink too much," I say, "it will dull your wits and you will play badly."

"A little mead always helps," he says. "It calms the nerves."

"Are you nervous?" I ask.

"Yes," he says. "Ever since…" He touches his neck again, where a scar should be but isn't. "Ever since I saw that grey place, I've felt as if something terrible is going to happen. As if something bad is coming."

"The Gravene," I say.

"What?"

"It is what the dead bandit said before I drew the light from him. Isn't it, Ethra?"

Ethra shrugs. "I heard nothing."

"What's the Gravene?" says Casmel.

"I don't know. The slite said it, too. Or something deep within it. 'It is coming. The

Gravene'. I don't know what it is, but they both said it."

"Maybe it's a good thing," says Ethra. "Why does it have to be bad? Maybe it's a new god come to bring us oatcakes, yellowberry pie and warm honeymilk. Gravene, the God of Sweet Things."

"I hope you're right," says Casmel, smiling but looking more than a little doubtful. Then he claps his hands. "Right! I'm off."

"What if you're not back by first light?" I ask as he's turning away.

"I'll be here. First light. Don't go without me. I can't get the coin I need to clear my father's debts without you, remember?"

I nod and watch as he walks from the copse and vanishes into the thickening woodland, heading toward Awlen.

"Are you sure you didn't hear the dead bandit speak?" I ask Ethra once Casmel has gone.

"Not so much as a death rattle. Not even a gurgle."

"It is not the God of Sweet Things, the Gravene," I say, more to myself than anything. "I am sure of that. If it is a god, at all."

Ethra yawns and I have to remind myself that she is a child of thirteen.

"Get some sleep," I say. "I'll keep first watch. I'll wake you when my eyes are too heavy for the task."

Four uneventful hours later, my eyelids feel like lead and I prod Ethra.

"You better take over," I say.

She tries to go back to sleep, but I snatch away her blanket and, grumbling incessantly, she takes my place.

I fall asleep so quickly it is as if I've been struck with a sap.

I dream of smoke. It is bitter and fragrant: pipegrass smoke. The smoke clears, and I see I am in a tavern. I can smell ale and mead and the sweat of men. It is noisy. There is music playing—sner strings and a bolla drum—and people laughing and arguing.

I look down and see my hands are not my own. They are holding spedig tiles.

I am Casmel. I am seeing through his eyes, hearing through his ears, smelling through his nose. He secures the tiles in one hand, tipping them toward himself—myself—and lifts a stone mug. He takes a drink. I smell it before I taste it. It smells of yeast, herbs and, to my mind, dirt. It tastes of all those things, but mostly of wet charcoal. He places the mug down and looks at the tiles again. I see his hand includes Foreg, the God of Deceits and Disguises. A good tile.

Will this happen with everyone I resurrect? Will I visit them in my dreams? Is that another part of my particular Glyst? I'm not sure I wish for it. What if I see something I do not wish to see? Like when I walked in on my mother and father because I had an earache, and they were 'wrestling', or so they told me. I notice, however, that it is different with Casmel. I have access to his senses, but not to his thoughts and feelings. With my father, I could feel his fear and understand his troubles. If this were my father playing spedig, I would know if his was a good hand or a loser's hand. I would know if the drink had shrunk his brain. With Casmel, I only know what he sees, hears, smells and tastes. I feel an itch on his shin—my shin?—and I feel him dismiss it with a rub of his heel.

I am suddenly very aware of every inch of his skin. Of its tightness to his lean frame. I feel his tongue lick his lips. I want to wake up and be out of his body. But, at the same time, I want to linger.

He looks up at the player opposite.

And what he sees, what *I* see, near stops my heart.

It is Slek Mydra.

He is holding no tiles. In front of him on the table is his sword. It is a Sceada's sword. A

horrible thing. It is short and wide. If you are
foolish enough to mock the length of a Sceada's
blade, they will say "It need only be as long as a
man's chest is deep" and then they will likely kill
you. There are barbs along the top of the blade. The
Sceada call these 'gut-thorns'. When the blade is
withdrawn from its unfortunate victim, the gut-
thorns snag on the entrails and viscera, dragging
them out to steam in the air. There are symbols
etched into the blade I do not recognise, and the
grip is bound in the same blood-red leather as its
owner's armour. The haft's pommel is a knot of
iron bristling with spikes.

"So," says Mydra in that soft, calm, almost
soothing voice of his, that somehow cuts through
the laughter and shouting, the sner strings and the
bolla drum. "Tell me what you know."

Casmel places his tiles face-down on the table. I
notice that his hands are trembling just a little.

"They are in a clearing, on the edge of town,"
he says. "If someone would be so kind as to bring
me a sheet of whitebark and a blackstick, I can
draw you a map. But let me see the coin first."

I awake with a violent jolt.

For a moment I think it was just a dream, a
nightmare. Casmel would never do such a thing.
But then I realise I know almost nothing about him.
What's more, the smell of the tavern lingers in my

nostrils and I can still taste the wet-charcoal tang of the ale. And then I remember the last thing he said to me before he left:

I can't get the coin I need to clear my father's debts without you, remember?

It wasn't a dream. It was real. Casmel has betrayed us.

"Ethra?"

She sits on the outer edge of the camp, leaning back against a tree, head lolling, fast asleep.

"Ethra!"

Her head snaps back, her eyes wide.

"I'm not asleep," she says. "I'm not. I wasn't. I'm wide awake." She sees the look of panic on my face. "What's wrong?"

"Casmel has betrayed us." I say. "He's sold our whereabouts to Slek Mydra."

"What? He wouldn't. Who's Slek Mydra? How do you know?" She rubs sleep from bleary eyes as she speaks.

"I saw through his eyes. It appears I can do that with someone I've resurrected."

"You saw through Cass's eyes?"

"The Scur's eyes, yes," I say. I don't want to call him by name anymore, do not want to think of him as Casmel Durn, brief ally. "I could see through my father's eyes after I brought him back from the Fields of Wealm."

"But Cass wouldn't. You gave his life back to him."

"He cares about nothing but coin," I say. "I wonder if his father has gambling debts, at all. It wouldn't surprise me to find that was a fiction to draw sympathy, so we would let down our guard and trust him."

I begin collecting our things together. After a minute's grumbling, Ethra helps me.

"Who's Slek Mydra?" she asks.

"A Sceada, captured in battle. He won his freedom in the Trial of Suswylt. The Jarl calls him 'Brother' now. He has been sent to find me. To kill me."

"A Sceada?" says Ethra, her face slackening with fear. "I have heard of the men of Scead. Brutes. They take joy in killing."

"What you've heard is true, and more and worse besides."

Ethra gathers her things at a quicker pace, and we are done in ten minutes.

"Do we leave Lata behind?" Ethra asks, as she climbs up behind me onto Skep. "What use is a second horse when I cannot ride?"

"No, she comes with us. She is too good-hearted for the Scur. Besides, he will have enough coin to buy himself a new horse." I set Skep in motion. Lata follows. "I hope his new mare kicks him in the head."

"I hope it, too," says Ethra. "Gedhearted pig." Then, a warble of nervousness in her voice. "Should we be travelling in the dark? Shouldn't we wait for first light?"

"And risk the Sceada finding us?"

Ethra actually shivers then and, for a moment, her skin loosens and looks like it is about to detach itself. But she makes her hands into fists, lets out a small angry sound and her flesh tightens.

"Let's go," she says with an air of impatience that suggests I was the one who raised concerns about travelling in the dark, that I'm the one who's afraid.

Of course, I *am* concerned. I *am* afraid. But I'm more afraid of Slek Mydra.

Then another fear strikes me so hard it forces a sharp intake of breath.

"What's wrong?" says Ethra.

"My father," I say. "The Scur told Mydra where we are, but he must also have confirmed *who* we are. Who *I* am."

"Oh," says Ethra.

I pull Skep to a halt.

I don't know what to do. Should I ride back to Gafol, warn my father? But what of Ethra? Perhaps we could ride back to El and ask her to warn my father, then continue on to the Dead City. My heart is drumming and my head is swirling with terrible thoughts and countless what-ifs and should-Is. I feel suddenly lightheaded. My hands tighten about Skep's reins. I am sure I am going to fall.

I take a breath.

Fear is in the lungs, I hear El saying. *It is not in the head or the heart, no matter how much it seems to be. It is in the lungs. It is in the breath. When you are afraid, breathe slowly through the nose. Take the air down deep into your lungs until it feels like it sits on top of your belly. Then let it out through your mouth, like you are blowing out a candle.*

The dizziness passes, and my heartbeat slows. My thoughts stop tripping over one another, separating out and becoming clearer.

"We ride on," I say, forgetting that Ethra has no idea why I stopped Skep in the first place or what that sharp intake of breath was about. "The Sceada will follow us. And as long as he is following us, he can't report back to the Jarl."

It's possible he could send someone back with a message, but I don't think so. The Sceada are single-minded. Mydra's every fibre will be devoted to finding me. Killing me. Honouring the Jarl. My father is safer if we keep moving forward.

Even if *we* are not.

Chapter 18

Swallowed by the Night

We have been travelling for an hour with what I estimate to be another hour to go before the darkness begins to lift, when I hear something in the pitch-clotted woods off to our left.

It is the sound of someone—or something—that does not want to be heard.

It is not the sound of an animal, not *just* an animal, anyway. It is the sound of a predator. My father has taught me the difference. An animal makes haphazard sounds, little clusters of sound. There might be brief pauses between those sounds but, on the whole, one sound follows another: a skitter of leaves, then another skitter of leaves, then the swish of a branch. When a predator makes a sound, such as I have just heard (the click of a snapping twig), that sound sits alone, as if the thing that has made it has become suddenly very still. It will be a full minute at least until it makes another sound. And that sound may be the last we hear.

"Ethra?" I whisper.

She has the good sense to whisper back, "Yes?"

"Something is following us. Off to the left. Maybe forty yards or so out. That's just beyond the range of my bow. So, it's either a clever human or a very clever beast."

"I don't think a clever person would be out in the woods in the dark," says Ethra. "Just idiots like us."

"True." Which means it is an animal. An intelligent animal. A predator.

I bring Skep to a halt. Lata wanders a few more paces then follows suit. I unshoulder my bow. Ethra leans back to give me the room I need. I move as slowly as I can, like a child playing scarecrows. If I move too quickly, the predator—and it *is* a predator, of that I have no doubt—will be alerted to my intentions. That could be a good thing. The predator might know its limitations and scarper. Or it might attack. I slide an arrow from my quiver.

I do not have the arrow nocked when I see the blackness between the trees, no more than ten yards ahead of me, *convulse*.

A nef.

It has the body of a wolf, but its forelegs are twice as long as the hind legs, making it look like it is rearing up. Its fur is glossy black and its hide is all folds and hanging swags. It looks as if it is wearing a wet, black cloak. It is its face, however, that is its most disturbing feature. Except for its huge split of a mouth, lined with gleaming-white, razor-sharp teeth, it has the face of a hairy, brutish man.

It launches itself at me.

I dig my heels into Skep, and he lurches forward.

Just enough that the nef misses us.

But Ethra is unprepared for the sudden movement and falls back off the horse, hands scrabbling at thin air. She hits the ground with a thud.

I jump down from Skep and slap the horse's rump, as much to clear the field of combat as put her out of harm's reach.

I see Ethra lying on her back, hands to her gut, gasping for air. Winded but otherwise uninjured, it would seem. The nef, already recovered from its disappointment, is advancing on her at speed.

In a single motion, I nock, draw, anchor and release. El would be proud.

My arrow strikes the nef's shoulder. I was aiming for the head. But it is enough to cause the creature to stop in its tracks. It lets out a howl almost as human as its face. It is a pitiable sound. But I don't have time for pity. I nock another arrow, draw, anchor and fire. This one strikes the nef above its all-too-human eye. It ceases its howling and collapses.

I run to Ethra.

"Are you okay?" I ask. "Nothing broken?"

"Just… winded…" she manages.

"We were lucky," I say. "So lucky." I point at the nef. It's still quivering as the last of the life goes out of it. "If one of us had been bitten…" I pull Ethra to her feet.

"If one of us had been bitten, what?"

"They have a poison gland just beneath the tongue. Their venom puts a darkness in the blood. Hallucinations, madness, rage, then death. It is a horrible thing."

"You know a lot about nef," says Ethra.

"My father said one of his cousins was nefbitten," I say, walking back toward Skep and Lata. "He said they had to put him to the sword, to end his suffering."

And then I remember something else that my father had told me about nef.

They hunt in pairs.

It is as if Ethra has been swallowed by the night. One moment, she is there. Then she is gone. The second nef has enveloped her in its swags of hide. It knows what it is doing. I cannot loose an arrow at it for fear of striking Ethra.

My father told me about this, too.

A lone nef will sometimes take a hostage. They are wily things. But know this, a hostage taken by a nef is already dead because the nef cannot resist the urge to bite. Do not be fooled. Do not withhold your blade or the tip of your arrow. Nef are clever and brutal. And you must be cleverer and more brutal.

Her voice muffled by the nef's black swaddling, Ethra cries, "Alys! Alys, please! I can't see! It has me!"

The nef's eyes flash briefly from the dark cloak that is its own hide. I can't help but see a smugness there, a challenge.

Ethra is already dead, I tell myself.

I nock an arrow.

The nef registers my decision, lets Ethra drop to the dirt and bounds toward the woods.

My first arrow strikes its hindquarters, and it barrels into a tree, howling that human howl. It gets back to its feet, braces to run again, but my second arrow strikes its chest with a resounding thud. But it doesn't fall. In fact, it seems suddenly filled with a frantic energy and charges at me.

Some nef, I hear my father say, *when they are facing death, will poison themselves. Nobody knows quite how they do it, but they take the darkness into their own blood. When they do this, they become something savage and lethal: a gasricnef.*

I put another arrow in its chest, but still it charges. I do not have time to nock another. I cast the bow aside and draw my sword. I have just enough time to sidestep the creature and swipe blindly at it as it passes. I feel my blade pass through the meat of its shoulder. It rolls into the undergrowth on the other side of the track, then lurches back to its feet and turns to face me.

I barely have time to plant my feet and ready my sword before it is charging again. Charging and *screaming* like a burnt child. Its mouth opens so wide I think—I hope—its head will split in two. It leaps at me and I thrust my sword forward, bracing for the impact. My blade slips into its chest as easily as if into water, and the full weight of the creature slams into me. Fortunately, the impact throws me clear of the nef and its gnashing, venom-wet teeth.

I jump to my feet, but my sword is no longer in my hands. It is buried to the hilt alongside my two arrows. And still the thing is bounding toward me, shrieking now. I wait until it is almost upon me, then dodge right. It slides past me, but only a couple of yards, then stops, turns and is bounding toward me again. I try to back away from it, at speed, and my heels catch on something and I am falling backwards.

The nef, the *gasricnef*, makes a sound very much like human laughter. It is the most frightening thing I've ever heard. It walks toward me now, seeming to take its time. That toothy slash of a mouth seems to be smiling. I use hands and feet and elbows to scuttle away from it as fast as I can but, even at its leisurely pace, it is closing the gap with ease.

When it is almost close enough to sink its teeth into my foot, I am struck by its stink. It smells sharp, acidic and like rotten pears. I am preparing to drive my foot into the pommel of my stolen sword, hoping despite the fact that it is already sunk up to the hilt, that I can drive it deeper, when the nef… stops. Stops laughing. Stops moving. And then it collapses, its slack hide pooling around it.

Behind the suddenly motionless nef Ethra is standing, but only just. Her sword protrudes from the beast's spine. I don't know if the blow was a lucky one or a strategic choice on Ethra's part. She doesn't look capable of a strategic decision. Or, indeed, any decision.

She is pale and sweaty, her eyes are glazed and her skin is rippling like water on the boil. Her left arm, the shirtsleeve ragged, is drenched in blood.

"Hallucinations, madness, rage," says Ethra. "Then death. It is a horrible thing."

Then she faints dead away.

Chapter 19

A Darkness in the Blood

I tend Ethra's injury as best I can with what medicinal herbs I have. The wound itself is surprisingly minor, a three-inch gash to the forearm, less than half-an-inch deep, but something in the nef's venom stops the blood from clotting and it bleeds profusely. I use all of my Marchweed and rosepulp as well as the Scur's supplies to get it under control. Our betrayer's herb bag also contains some mamera leaf, doubtless to be smoked for non-remedial purposes, and I wake Ethra long enough to get her to chew on it. It should help with the pain and fever. Heat is pouring from her, as if she has burning firewood for bones.

I put her in front of me on Skep, my cloak looped round both our waists to keep her secure. There are no signs of any pursuers, and I am able to stop every two hours to clean her wound and administer more mamera. Each occasion I tend the nef bite, it looks worse. By the time I stop for the night and set-up camp, it is oozing puss and the entire arm is as red as the rosepulp I've been administering to slow the bleeding. Her skin hasn't stopped rippling since the attack.

I am preparing more mamera when Ethra says, "You will have to kill me."

I have become so accustomed to the silence, I jump and the leaves scatter.

Ethra is lying on her side, looking at me, just her face peeking out of her blanket.

"You should sleep," I say.

"My blood hurts," she says.

"I know. I'll give you more mamera. It will help a little."

"A little, but not enough," she scowls.

"It's all I have."

"I'm going to die, anyway. A horrible death. You said so yourself. Kill me quickly. And then you can bring me back using your Glyst."

I have done little but think about this option since I first dressed her wound.

"I don't know if I can, Ethra."

"You brought back your father and Cass. Why not me?"

"I meant that I don't know if I can kill you."

"Why not? You killed the Leccans and the bandits."

"It is different to kill in combat. And even that I do not find easy."

"Will it be easier to watch me suffer?" Her skin ripples violently then, a sail caught in a strong headwind, and her face stretches and bulges grotesquely.

"Of course not."

"Then do it."

"Take some more mamera," I say, collecting the leaves from the ground. "Sleep a little more and then we will talk about it."

"I am going to die, anyway. You could make it painless."

"I know," I say. "Let me think on it."

After a brief silence in which I think she has fallen asleep, she says, "How many days?"

"What?"

"How many days will it take me to die? How many days of pain?"

"Just three or four. Five at the most."

I am lying, of course. When my father put his nefbitten cousin to the sword, he had been raging for a fortnight. I don't know how much longer he would have suffered if he had not been granted mercy.

Ethra is relentless for the entire journey the next day. Whenever she is conscious, she asks me why I have not killed her yet, why I am happy to see her suffer. I am relieved whenever she loses consciousness.

There is no clearing in which to make our camp, and night comes at us quickly, so we sit facing each other, just a few yards apart, leaning back against the thin, grey trees that are all this part of the world has to offer. I don't know what type of tree they are. They look like sickly old men. In truth, I'm not sure what part of the world we are in. I *think* I have kept us moving eastwards. I *think* we are moving parallel to the Fisher Road, but it has been at least six hours since I've heard the sound of people.

"You are right, Slek Mydra," says Ethra suddenly, looking up and past me. "I should kill her."

I stand, turn, draw my sword. My head is spinning, my heart striking my sternum so hard it hurts.

There is nobody there.

Hallucinations, I think. Madness. Rage.

When I turn back, Ethra is gone.

"Ethra? You need to stay with me. When you die, I can bring you back. We can hunt an animal, something big. I can take its lifelight and put it in you. But I can't do that if you are not with me."

"You're a liar!" The voice comes out of the sickly woods, but I can't tell from which direction. "My father is here with me. He says so. He says you are a liar! He says I will suffer for weeks before the relief of death finds me. *Weeks*, he says.

But his face is a nest of hungry, featherless birds, and I'm not certain I can trust him."

"That is the nefbite talking," I say. "Come back here. I will give you some mamera. You will feel a little better."

"Mamera does not touch the fire in my bones. Nor the darkness in my blood."

I still can't tell from which direction her voice is coming. But there is a wispy quality to it I recognise. She has shed her skin. Then I realise why it is I'm struggling to locate Ethra from the sound of her voice.

It is coming from somewhere above me.

I look up, but it is too late. She is swooping down at me from the feeble canopy, stars scattered behind her. Her glove-like hand is wrapped about a rock. I see it blur toward me.

My eyes peel apart. I can taste blood. I try to move, but my hands are tied behind me. For a moment, I think I am still a prisoner of the Scur and that everything else—the bandits, the betrayal at Awlen, the nef—has been a dream.

Ethra sits opposite me, leaning back against one of the old-man trees. At least her body is, red and glistening.

"We can't kill you," she says. "Who will 'ring us 'ack to life?"

"Yes," says a wispy voice. "It is complicated."

Skin-Ethra hangs in the air above her flayed counterpart. The infection in her wound has spread. That entire boneless arm is red. The wound drips pus. I hear it *pat-pat* on the dead leaves of the forest floor.

"I'n not sure I want to 'e 'rought 'ack to life," says Body-Ethra.

"Yes," says Skin-Ethra. "It has not been a good life. It already feels as if it has gone on far too long. When did we leave your aunty's roundhouse?"

"A few days ago."

Skin-Ethra and Body-Ethra laugh in unison.

"No, no," says Body-Ethra. "It has 'een at least a *year*. Silly girl!"

"At least," says Skin-Ethra. "I am fourteen now. I remember my birthday. You made me honeyed oatcakes and strawberries. And you gave me a necklace made of shiny metal and gleaming gemstones." Her infected hand moves up to her neck and feels about. "Now, where has it gone?"

"I did not give you a necklace, Ethra. It has been only a few days since we set out to take you to Utlath. You are still thirteen. There was no birthday."

"Liar!" she says, floating down to hover an inch from the ground, a yard or so from me. "You stole it!"

"What?" My forehead is throbbing where she struck me with the rock.

"The necklace. You must have stolen it!"

"There was no—"

She slaps me. It is like being struck with a piece of leather.

"Liar!" she says.

"She's a liar and a thief," says Body-Ethra. "Sla' her 'ace again."

Skin-Ethra slaps me again. My face feels like it has been stung by a straggis wasp, and there are tears in my eyes.

"Stop it, Ethra! It is the nef's venom that is making you—"

She slaps me again.

And I start to cry. I am ashamed. I haven't cried since the Ritual of the Seven Cuts and the Seven Cups. That something as silly as a few slaps should bring me to tears feels somehow unjust. But, by Wyrchen, the God of Pain, it *hurts*. But it isn't just the pain; it's the cruelty and the humiliation.

"Again," says Body-Ethra. "Harder this ti'."

Skin-Ethra raises a hand again but does not slap me. Her face, rippling and empty, somehow takes on an aspect of sadness. Her hand drops to her side.

"Sla' her!" cries Body-Ethra.

"No," says Skin-Ethra. "She is sad now. I have made her sad. And that makes my heart ache. I am sorry, Alys. I don't know what's wrong with me."

"It's the nef's bite," I say. "It isn't your fault."

"You're an idiot, that's what's wrong with you!" says Body-Ethra rising. "And you don't have a heart." She beats her chest. "I have a heart. You are just a nothing with a skin on it. A skin on it like a 'ilk 'udding."

Body-Ethra strides toward me, drawing her knife from her belt.

"I will cut her. I will give her so'thing to cry a'out."

Skin-Ethra's hand snakes out and coils around the muscle and sinew of Body-Ethra's wrist.

"No," she says. "Enough. We should sleep. We are tired. Mamma says that when we are tired we get grumpy."

"I'n not tired!" shrieks Body-Ethra. "And I'n not grunky! *You're* grunky! Get off 'e! You're just trousers and a tunic!"

"You're a naked idiot! I have all the sense!"

And then the two of them are fighting, rolling around in the dirt. The knife flies from Body-Ethra's hand and lands at my feet. I use my heels to scrape it toward me, then turn on my bottom so I can grab it with my hands. I don't know how much time I have, so I get to cutting immediately.

"You have to go back inside," says Skin-Ethra. "You can't be trusted to behave well outside. You've embarrassed yourself."

"You've engarrassed *yourself*," snaps Body-Ethra, but her voice sounds muffled.

Skin-Ethra is slowly slithering back into place.

The blade cuts through my bonds, but I keep my hands behind my back, gripping the knife.

Ethra—Whole-Ethra—stands, dusting herself off. She looks at me with such fear and desperation, my heart breaks.

"Make it stop," she says. "Everything hurts! Please kill me. While you can. While I can let you. Or my blood will become darkness again and I'll hurt you. And then who'll kill me? And who will bring me back?"

I stand, letting her see that my hands are free, letting her see the knife.

"Okay," I say. "Okay. But we need to find something I can pull the lifelight from. A big animal."

"Cass," says Ethra, looking past me, eyes wide.

"You are hallucinating, Ethra. The nef's bite—"

"Cass," she says again, pointing now.

"Ethra," says a voice behind me. "Alys."

I turn.

It is him. The Scur. Casmel Durn.

I glare at him.

"Well, Ethra," I say. "We needn't hunt for a big animal. We have one right here."

Chapter 20

Tracked

"Why didn't you wait?" he says, walking over to me with a look of betrayal on his face.

Betrayal. On *his* face.

I slash at him with the knife. But anger makes me brutish and clumsy. Lucky for the Scur. He grabs my wrist and stays the blade an inch from his neck. My other hand knots into a fist and I punch him hard in the chin. His head snaps back, and he rocks on his heels. He manages to remain standing, but he is off balance. I drive my foot into the side of his knee and he crumples, releasing my wrist as he drops.

"What in the name of Memynd?" he says, teeth gritted against the pain.

He scuttles back as I advance on him, my own teeth gritted, the knife held so tightly in my hand my knuckles are blanched white.

"Memynd?" I say. "The God of Madness? Try Foreg, the God of Deceits and Disguises, you gedhearted foorstig!"

"What? I returned to the camp, and you were gone."

"We were gone? Of *course* we were gone. You betrayed us. You betrayed us to Slek Mydra. And for what? For coin. For your oh-so-precious coin."

"How? How did you—"

"How did I know? I *saw*. I saw through your eyes. I heard through your ears." I toss the knife from hand to hand. "We need an animal to save Ethra. And you're it."

"Ethra? What's—"

"She is nefbitten. But what do you care? You condemned us to a different death, that's all. At the hands of the Sceada."

"Nefbitten…" He looks at Ethra and manages to conjure an expression of concern that would easily have fooled someone who wasn't fully aware of precisely the kind of man he was.

"Look," he says, holding his hands out, placating, surrendering. "Just listen. I don't know how you think you know—"

"I don't *think* I know. I know. It is part of my Glyst. When I dream, I can see through the eyes of those I have brought back to life. My father. You." I let out a growl of rage. "To think, I *saved* you. And you repaid me with betrayal."

"I didn't betray you. Just listen."

I take a deep breath, still tossing the knife from hand to hand.

"You have one minute," I say. "One minute. Ethra?"

"Yes?" she says. Her voice sounds weak. I glance back. She's sat at the base of the tree where I was bound, her knees drawn up to her chest, her eyes drooping with exhaustion.

"Count down from one minute. In your head. When you get to zero, say 'kill the gedhearted foorstig'."

"Okay," she says.

I think she might be asleep before she reaches zero.

I turn back to the Scur.

"Talk," I say.

"I was looking for a game," he says, talking quickly. "There are a few taverns in Awlen, but most of them had tyndle games going, not spedig, so it took a while. And while I was wandering the streets, I heard talk of men from Gafol, four of them, one a Sceada, looking for a pair of Glysters. I asked an old street-cutler if they'd found the Glysters yet, these men from Gafol, and he said they were giving up on the town soon and would be searching the outlying woods. I let it be known I'd seen you. Then I went to my spedig game. I knew word would get to your pursuers sooner or later. And sure enough it did—"

"You're not helping yourself," I say. "You're just confirming what I already know."

"Let me finish. You said you'd listen."

"Go on. You're running out of time."

"You're slowing me down!"

"Then hurry up!"

"The one you talked about, the Sceada, sits down at the table. And tells me to talk. And I say—"

"You tell him we are in a clearing on the edge of town. You ask for someone to bring you a sheet of whitebark and a blackstick, so you can draw a map. But first, of course, you ask to see the coin, your reward for our betrayal."

"Yes. Well, not the betrayal. But everything else."

"*Not* the betrayal? How can you say you didn't betray us? You *drew a map*!"

"And, if you were looking through my eyes, you'd have seen the map. You'd have seen I drew a map pointing them to the southern edge of town, putting you as far from where you were actually camped as I could."

I loosen my grip on the knife. Colour returns to my knuckles.

"I did not see the map."

"You didn't see the map? I thought you were looking 'through my eyes'. I thought you saw what I saw."

"I woke up at that point."

"You 'woke up'?"

"Yes. I thought you had betrayed us."

"Betrayed you? I put my life in danger." He is standing now, brushing dirt and leaves from his clothes. "Do you have any idea what it was like to sit in front of the Sceada and lie, and think all the while he *knows* I am lying? Did you see his sword at least? It would have dragged my guts out onto the table. They would have been the last thing I saw." His face is reddening with anger now. "And then I had to calmly finish my game of spedig, collect my winnings, pick up enough supplies for our return journey." He points to two bags leaning against a nearby tree, one his, one larger and bulging. "I had to do this knowing that the Sceada—the Sceada with his disembowelling blade and his quiet, reasonable voice—is going to realise very soon that I have tricked him. Not because he doesn't find you, that would give me plenty of time, a fruitless search like that, but because the map I drew doesn't match the landscape of the southern edge of Awlen because I have *never seen* the southern edge of Awlen. And when I get back to our camp, *our* camp, you have gone. And taken my horse, no less! I had to follow you on foot. I travelled day and night, hardly sleeping."

Only now do I really notice his physical appearance. He is scratched and grimy, dark crescents hang beneath his eyes. His clothes are torn and muddy.

"I didn't see the map," I say, looking down at my boots.

"You didn't see the map."

"It isn't my fault I awoke. I did not choose to."

"But you chose to believe that I had betrayed you."

"You have to understand how it looked…"

"I understand only that you think I am the worst kind of person."

"You were going to take me back to Gafol to die," I say, attempting to turn the tables. "You only chose to accompany us to the Dead City because there was an opportunity to accumulate more of your precious coin."

"Well… yes, but…"

"Don't pretend you are any less the person who tried to sap me at the roadside, Casmel Durn."

"Cass," he says. "Only my mother calls me Casmel. Or did." He sags with a weariness I understand. My bones ache, too. And my muscles.

Behind me, Ethra moans.

"We can berate each other later," he says. "Neither of us has emerged from this with a heroic sheen. We need to do something about Ethra. She is… billowing."

I turn and see he's right. She is standing now, and her skin is detaching. Her mouth is stretched in a wide and silent scream.

"We need a big animal," I say. "You wait here with Ethra. You may need to bind her. I'll see what I can find in the woods."

"Why didn't you use the nef?" says Casmel.

"I should have," I say. "But it would have meant putting Ethra to the sword. It would have meant killing her. And I… couldn't. Not then."

"And now?"

"What choice do I have?" I say. "I just hope there are some large creatures here about that aren't nef."

"Actually," says Casmel, and there is more than a hint of contrition in his voice. "There's a bit of a problem."

"A problem?"

"Well, it might actually be more in the way of a solution, given our current predicament."

"Your words are clear as clay, Casmel."

"I am being followed. Tracked, to be more precise."

"Followed?" My stomach seems to tighten and loosen in the same instant. "Slek Mydra?"

"No. Two men from Gafol."

"If they have a grefa stone, we will hear it long before they reach us," I say.

"They are not using grefa stones," says Casmel. "One is a tracker and one they call 'the slaughterman'."

I know immediately who the men are. This 'slaughterman' is Eftas Hilder. The tracker is doubtless Chayn Syrunn, the best huntsman in Gafol and the Jarl's brother-in-law. The only advantage Syrunn offers us is his advancing years. While his stalking skills have only grown sharper with time, his legs are beginning to slow. Both men, Hilder and Syrunn, are known for their unpleasantness. Hilder's is, in its way, a more palatable sort. He is simply a brute. Syrunn, on the other hand, is known for his cruelty. I remember something my mother told me about him:

It is an acceptable thing to take pleasure in the hunt, even in the kill, because there is skill in it. But Syrunn enjoys the pain. Your father says he will delay the killing stroke for as long as possible. He takes delight in the beast's suffering. There is nef venom in that man's heart. Even the Sceada are not so poisoned. They inflict pain because they want to be feared. To be feared in combat is an advantage. It is a practical thing. With Syrunn, it is a perversion.

"How far behind are they?" I ask.

"A couple of hours, I think."

"You *think*?"

"I'm not at my best, Alys. I'm tired and have recently been punched in the face."

"We haven't time for your self-pity," I say. "Ethra is—"

"Self-pity, you've got to be—"

Ethra lets out a moan of pain that turns to a hiss.

"We haven't *time*, Casmel" I say. "We need to set a trap." And then I say, "Oh."

Because there appears to be an arrow through my leg.

Chapter 21

Stalker and Slaughterman

The moment I see it, the injury erupts with pain. I drop my knife and both hands go to the arrow's shaft.

Casmel, having seen the arrow land, drops to the ground and rolls left.

It is a wise move. An arrow cuts the air where he was just standing and sinks into the trunk of one of the old-men trees behind me.

Now that Casmel isn't blocking my view, I can see Syrunn and Hilder. Both have already nocked fresh arrows and are drawing their bowstrings. And both are tracking Casmel with their arrow points as he darts between the trees. I wonder why one of them isn't taking aim at me, then realise they intend to take me alive. That's why they didn't take down Casmel first. That would have alerted me to their presence, and I may have had time to do what Casmel is doing right now. Namely, scarpering.

Hilder looses his arrow, then Syrunn. Both fail to find their target.

"Go after him," says Syrunn.

Hilder does as he's told.

Syrunn shoulders his bow, draws his sword and strides toward me.

I reach for the knife, but pain has me dizzy and disoriented, and the huntsman kicks the blade away with ease. It lands several yards away. He puts the edge of his sword to my throat and, with his other hand, grabs the arrow shaft and twists it.

I cry out.

He grins.

"You're going to do as your told, girlie, aren't you?"

"Yes," I manage. The pain is so severe, I am almost blinded by it.

"Good." He gives the arrow another twist, then lets go. "Good."

"Durn!" he shouts. "If you would hear her scream, carry on running into the woods!"

He cups a hand to his ear and makes a performance of listening for Casmel's reply. There is blood on that hand. Mine.

"No, boy? Don't believe me?"

He twists the arrow again.

I scream.

Ethra moans.

"Who is screaming?" she says. "Is it me?"

Syrunn lets go of the arrow, and I drop to the floor.

I watch as the huntsman walks toward Ethra with a lightness of step that is grotesque, as if he is barely suppressing the urge to dance.

"You are the other Glystgedder," he says. "You are not required. Mydra has no interest in you."

And then he drives his sword into her chest, up to the hilt.

I try to cry out Ethra's name, but my mouth and throat are suddenly too dry.

Ethra doesn't have time to scream. Her skin billows outward once, then hangs slack and lifeless, the skin of someone three times her size. She collapses back against the tree, skin trailing for a moment like loose clothing.

"Vile thing!" Syrunn says, staggering back, his voice thick with disgust. "Vile." Then, as if Ethra's death is of no consequence, he shouts again, "Durn! Would you hear her scream?"

"No, I wouldn't." Casmel's voice comes from the opposite direction from which he ran. Somehow he has circled round. Over the roar of blood in my ears, I can hear Hilder crashing through the undergrowth on a fool's errand. Casmel has his sword drawn and is walking toward the huntsman.

Syrunn's blade goes to my throat.

"Another step and she will bleed out here in this paltry excuse for a forest."

Casmel stops walking.

"Now drop the blade," says Syrunn.

Casmel doesn't drop his sword.

"Drop it," says Syrunn. He digs the tip of his own blade into the meat of my neck.

Casmel drops his sword.

At the very moment his blade hits the ground, Hilder appears not far from where he blundered after Casmel.

"I can't f—" he begins. "There he is!" He actually points at Casmel, as if it isn't perfectly obvious to everyone precisely where Casmel 'is'. He nocks an arrow and draws back his bowstring.

"I wouldn't," says Casmel.

"Wouldn't what?" says Hilder.

"Kill me."

"And why wouldn't I do that, you little gedstain?"

"Because I'm the only one who can control her." Casmel looks at me. "I'm the only one who can stop her from killing all of us."

Hilder glances at me and sneers.

"Her?" he says. "Kill us all? And how exactly would she do that?" He pulls the bowstring back to the anchor point.

"Wait," says Syrunn, holding one hand up to Hilder. "If she's so dangerous, maybe I should just kill her now."

"And release more spores?" says Casmel, taking a step back. "Haven't you done enough damage?"

"What?" says Syrunn.

"It's a wonder you haven't started losing your skins already," says Casmel. "Cover your mouths. Have you no sense?"

"What's the idiot talking about?" says Hilder. "What's he going on about, losing our skins?"

"Do you want to end up like her?" says Casmel, pointing at Ethra.

Hilder notices her for the first time. His eyes widen in horror.

Casmel points to Syrunn's hand, the one that had gripped the shaft of the arrow. The one he had cupped to his ear.

"Tell me that isn't the Glyster's blood," he says.

Syrunn looks at his hand, then wipes it on the leg of his trousers.

"It's too late for that," says Casmel. "The spores will be in you now." He turns to me. "Alys, you mustn't use your Glyst for ill. It is against the wishes of Fryth." He turns back to Syrunn. "Fryth is her household's god. Fryth, the God of Peace?"

"I know who Fryth is," says Syrunn, staring at his hand, then wiping it again, harder, on his trousers.

"As long as she keeps Fryth at the centre of her thoughts, she will not transmute the spores."

"Transmute the spores?" says Syrunn, looking warily at me as he speaks.

"I don't know how it works," says Casmel. "But, somehow, the spores become as the breath of a giant, of a god even, and... well..." He points at Ethra again. "*That* happens."

While the stalker and the slaughterman are looking at Ethra's corpse, Casmel takes a very slight step forward and slides his foot under his dropped sword, where the blade meets the hilt. He knows this prattle can't convince them for long.

"And why would she listen to you?" Hilder demands.

"The Glyst has driven her mad. She believes I am Luthyl, emissary of Fryth. The Spirit of Love."

If I weren't in so much pain, I would laugh. Luthyl? The Spirit of Love? Where do these silly confections spring from?

"She will do as I say," Casmel continues. "So long as her life isn't threatened. I cannot control her if she is afraid. It is bad enough that she is in pain."

Syrunn scrutinises Casmel. His eyes narrow with suspicion, but the blade moves away from my neck.

"I think you play a game with us," says Syrunn. "I think you are still at the spedig table in Awlen, and your hand is poor."

Casmel points at Ethra again.

"I wish it were so."

Syrunn's eyes narrow to slits.

"If I kill her," he says. "How will she 'transmute' these spores you're expecting us to believe in?"

"Well... it's more that she's *stopping* them from transmuting right now. The spores? The Glystspores? They have a will of their own, you see. They wish to be as the breath of a god. Alys is the only thing stopping them. And I—by which I mean, Luthyl, the Spirit of Love—I am the only thing stopping her. Which is why I cannot let her sleep. Why do you think she looks so grotesque with sleeplessness, her eyes all puffy and blood-tinted, like a suffocating bladderfish? She hasn't slept in days."

I let out a yelp of pain.

"Luthyl!" I cry. "I am in agony! I cannot control the spores!"

I *am* in agony and, were there spores to control, I almost certainly would not be able to do so.

"You need to put something on the wound. I have a battle poultice in my bag. It has rosepulp, Marchweed and mamera in it."

"If you are treating us as spedig tiles," says Syrunn, "I will cut a hole in you, fill it with dirt and watch you die in agony for *hours*. Hilder? Keep your arrow-point on him."

Syrunn walks to the bags, keeping wide of Casmel.

"The larger of the two," says Casmel. "It is in a green oilcloth."

Syrunn empties the bag onto the forest floor and kicks the contents about until he finds the green package. Once he has the mamera leaves, he strides back toward me.

"Girlie," he says. "This is going to hurt."

He kneels down next to me and, without warning, grips the shaft of the arrow where it has passed through my leg.

I scream.

"I told you you'd hear her scream, boy," says Syrunn and pulls the arrow through my leg.

I feel every inch of its shaft, the grains in the wood, and the fletching, as if a flock of birds is passing through the wound. I scream again. Or, perhaps, it is the same scream continued.

I know only that I have lost consciousness when I find myself crawling out of the darkness, drawn by the sweet scent of rosepulp and the heady aroma of mamera. I can only have been absent for less than a minute because Syrunn is still applying the poultice. I blink tears from my eyes and look across at Casmel.

"Don't be so dramatic, Alys," he says. "It was just one arrow. Not an entire *quiver* of them." He widens his eyes on the word 'quiver'.

I am too dizzy with pain to catch his meaning at first.

Then it comes to me.

An entire quiver of arrows. On my back.

I look down at Syrunn. He is busy with the poultice. I glance across at Hilder. His attention is entirely on Casmel.

I feel unconsciousness threatening again.

I grit my teeth against it, as I did during the Ritual of the Seven Cuts and the Seven Cups. This is just *one* cut, I tell myself, and it *will not* best me.

In a single fluid motion, I take an arrow from my quiver and shove it into Syrunn's neck. He snaps upright, shock in his eyes, his hand going to the arrow and pulling it out. There is blood, but not as much as there ought to be. I realise I hadn't the strength to deliver a killing blow.

Casmel scoops his sword up into the air with his foot. But fails to catch it. I see his face fall slack with dread. He knows Hilder's arrow will find him.

With my good leg, I lash out at Syrunn. The flat of my foot catches his hip and he staggers away from me, still staring in disbelief at the bloody arrow in his hand.

And then he has another arrow, this one in the side of his head. Hilder's arrow.

"Ged!" the slaughterman barks, and he begins to nock another arrow.

Casmel grabs his sword and sidesteps, putting Syrunn between himself and Hilder. He barges into Syrunn, sending him flailing toward Hilder. The stalker and the slaughterman go down in a thrashing of limbs.

Hilder kicks his way out from under the now-shrieking Syrunn. His sword is only half unsheathed when Casmel puts his blade into his chest. And then Syrunn jerks upward and is somehow standing, his eyes looking in opposite directions, his face a bloody mask, shrieking still. He scrabbles at his belt for his knife, almost finds it, then collapses face-first into the dirt and leaves, his shrieking muffled for a few seconds before ceasing entirely.

"Eyes all puffy and blood-tinted, like a suffocating bladderfish?" I say and lose consciousness once more.

Chapter 22

Resurrections

"Alys."

I open my eyes and see Casmel staring down at me, just for a second, then I black out again.

"Alys!"

I open my eyes again and force them to stay open this time.

"I don't know how long we've got to help Ethra. I know you're very tired and you can sleep soon, I promise, but for now you need to shake yourself awake. Here, drink this."

He pours a little water into my mouth, and I manage to swallow it without choking.

"Now let's get you up," he says, looping an arm around my waist and lifting me. "Don't put any weight on that gammy leg, mind."

I want to tell him I'm not stupid, but I can't summon the energy to speak.

He guides me over to Ethra.

The sight of her jolts me awake more effectively than any herbalist's tonic. A glassy eye stares at me from a bed of muscle through a distorted hole in a face too big but still horribly familiar. Only it doesn't stare, that eye. It is already becoming milky.

"Is it too late?" asks Casmel, his arm still around my waist.

"I don't know," I say. "Sit me down next to her."

Casmel lowers me gently to the ground. I look at Ethra's slack and lifeless face. I try to find an ember of rage, a spark of fury, something that might start a fire inside me, an inferno. But there is only the ache of sadness, the numbness of loss, as I felt when my mother died.

"It only works when I'm angry," I say. "And my anger is smothered with sadness."

"But it's still there," says Casmel, sitting down next to me. His voice is quiet, reflective. "It never goes away. Mine doesn't, at least. Sometimes, it seems it has, when I am laughing and living, when I am winning. But I never have to look hard to find it again. And, for some stupid reason, I can't *help* looking for it. I'm like a child who can't stop picking at a scab until it bleeds afresh. If you're like me, your anger will still be there. It might *always* be there. It is the same with sadness, and with fear. They lurk and skulk."

"I'm not like you," I say, without thinking.

"No," he replies. "Fair enough. You are not like me in many ways. But in this, I suspect we are the same. I suspect we are all the same."

I am about to dismiss him again when I remember El saying:

Listen when a person talks. Always. Think on what they say. Even if it seems like horseged at first. There may be something *in it of value. Even horseged can help the roses thrive.*

"I am afraid most of the time," I say. "Even when I appear not to be. The morning I went hunting with my father, when the slite attacked and my Glyst let itself be known, I was thinking about that. About how I bury my fear like a crow buries its food. It was not so before the Ritual of the Seven Cuts and the Seven Cups. Only since. It was as if I bled courage into each of those cups."

"My father was like that, when he came back from the Battle of Thelland. He jumped at shadows and cried in his sleep. When he wasn't crying or jumping or sleeping, he raged. Anger and fear sit very close to one another. They intertwine like trees planted too close together."

I look at him, but his eyes are fixed in the distance, or in the past.

Anger and fear sit very close to one another.

I cannot find the anger, but the fear, as always, is easy to find. I bury it like a crow buries its food, and a crow does not bury its food deep. It sits, my fear, in my belly, like a too-heavy meal. I examine it. It is mostly a thing of acids and oils. It is greasy and it burns. If it were a creature, it would be a fensnake. They are an unpleasant yellow colour with a venom that causes bloody vomiting, and they live in the slimiest waters.

"Hello, Master Fensnake," I say.

"What?" says Casmel, but I ignore him.

At first, I see Master Fensnake as coiled up tightly in my belly. Sitting there, heavy and pleased with himself. But then, I realise that is not the case. My belly is just where the largest portion of him sits. The upper length of his body rears up, as he would were he about to strike. He reaches as far as my head. My brain. My mind. That is where the worst of him is, the bit with the fangs and the venom, inside my mind. But between gut and head is my heart, around which Master Fensnake has made a knot of himself. And inside that knot is an ember, its heat largely hidden by the competing coolness of the fensnake's body.

My anger.

I reach out with my mind and loosen Master Fensnake's knot, as I would a bowstring that needs adjusting. The worst of him, the portion in my mind, *hisses* and shows his dripping fangs. I surprise myself by finding I am able to ignore its threat so long as I concentrate on the business of loosening the knot.

The knot falls slack and the heat of my anger escapes in a wave, in a pulse.

It spreads out from my chest, through my limbs and down to my fingertips and the tips of my toes. I even feel a little of it pass from the wound in my leg, and it is a strangely satisfying pain.

All thoughts of snakes and knots and embers fall away, all those abstracts, and I am pushing my hands into Ethra's wound. It is cold, the blood thickened to a tackiness. But there is a hiss nevertheless, and ribbons of steam coil upwards. I feel Casmel shuffle away from me. Ethra's flesh billows a little.

And then I am in the Nowhere once more, that place of troublelessness where it would be so tempting to stay.

But the ripple comes, as it did before.

The stone has hit the lake.

It is a about the Big Things. The Gods.

Suddenly, I am back in the forest of frail, old-man trees, still haloed by the steam from Ethra's blood.

I turn to the lifeless form of Chayn Syrunn, pointing my bloody right hand at him, the left pushed harder into Ethra's wound.

"It is coming," says Syrunn's dead, motionless mouth. "It is coming. The Gravene."

"Yes, yes," I say. "The *Gravene* is coming. I know. I know. Don't the dead ever stop going on and on about it?"

The pale-pink lifelight lifts from Syrunn's head. His body collapses a moment later, as if everything beneath the flesh has been in the grave six months.

The light floats toward me. The scent of blackberries and rose petals swirls in the air. I reach out and touch the light.

And then Ethra is looking down at me, smiling.

"It is gone," she says. "The darkness. It is gone from my blood." Then her brow knits with concern. "But what are we going to do with you? You look terrible."

"Like a suffocating bladderfish?" I ask.

"A little," says Ethra.

I sit up, wincing as the wound in my thigh ignites.

"Where's Cass?" I ask.

"He has gone to get something. He said he has a plan."

"Gone to get what? What plan?"

"He didn't say. He just said it would be up to you."

"Up to me?"

"If you were able."

"Able to do what?"

Ethra shrugs. Then she shivers and I see a little fear in her eyes.

"What's wrong?" I ask.

"It was as Cass described it," she says. "There were no Unrim, and there was no River of Honey. It was here, but colourless. Tiny grey mushrooms sprouted from everything. I could feel them on my tongue. I could feel them under my eyelids when I blinked. It was silent. The silence of being underwater. And there were skinny people-things with holes instead of faces, and they were made of sticky smoke, as when a fatty animal burns." She looks at me. "What is that place, Alys?"

"I don't know," I say. "I have not seen it."

"You are lucky. It will stay in my head for some time, I think. For a long time."

I hear someone approach.

Casmel emerges near to where he darted into the woods when he was being pursued by Hilder. He is carrying my bow, and my quiver is on his back. In his other hand is a rather poor example of a welpa.

I point at the welpa and say, "We can't risk a fire. Besides, that thing has barely enough meat for its own purposes."

"It's all I could manage in the time," he says. "Anyway, we're not going to eat it." He looks at me with concern, then. "But you do not have to do this if you haven't the strength or the inclination."

"Do what?"

"I have a plan," he says and grins.

Chapter 23

Angenga

Hilder opens his eyes and screams.

He screams for a long time. Until, in fact, Casmel places a hand over his mouth and says, "Hush, slaughterman. Enough of that now."

"I was dead," he says. "I was dead. You put your sword in me."

"Yes, I did," says Casmel. "I'd apologise, but you *were* trying to kill me."

Hilder tries to launch himself at Casmel, at which point he realises he is bound, hands behind his back, to the tree behind him.

"Let me loose," he says. "Fight me like a man. I will—" His mouth hangs open and a look of horror stiffens his face. I have never seen an expression on the slaughterman's face other than stupidity or meanness, and it is troubling. "I was dead. And I was… what was that place?"

"Never mind 'that place'," says Casmel. "It is only where you belong. We have a message for Slek Mydra."

"Never mind?" says Hilder. "Never mind? It is in my head now and forever. I can still taste it. It tasted as it looked, grey and damp. And… those things. Those *things*. Like people, but as if made of… *ligaments*. And… oh blessed Fryth… they came for me and they dragged me through the woods—through *these* woods but with all colour bled out—and they took me to a circle of stones, like the Wyrsan Stones that stand at the heart of the Freewood, and they threw me in the middle, kicking and punching me. They bound and pegged me to the ground, face to the sky." He strains at his bonds again. "Untie me! Please, untie me!"

"No," says Casmel. "Now, stop blathering and listen. A message for Slek Mydra."

"The sky," Hilder continues, as if Casmel has not even spoken. "The sky, it was not right. It was as milk curdled by a drop of vinegar. Pale and clotted, thick here, thin there. And there were things moving through those thin parts, like fish but also like snakes and like spiders but of one body. The ligament-people started dancing and singing. The singing was horrible, so high it drilled into my ears, and the words gibberish. They danced like they were afire. And then…" He begins to shake now, and for a moment I think he is trying to demonstrate the dance of the ligament-people. "And then… oh blessed Fryth… that curdled sky parted and… *it* came. *It*. It was vast. The colour of an old man's milky eye. It had no shape but was filled with teeth and claws and rats' tails, and it turned and turned like a boiling stew, and there was something like guts, like bowels, and they were translucent… and I could see… *people*… people in them straining to get out. And. And. And."

Casmel slaps him then.

Hilder glares at him, straining against his bonds again. But it is obvious to me that even were he to free himself, he would be no threat. He's weak. Even his build is diminished. His clothes hang loose, like Ethra's flesh when she lay lifeless. And there is something lifeless about him, too. He is pale and drawn. His eyes are yellow where they should be white. I remember one Wealdnight, when Roisa and I were just seven or eight, we tried to scare each other with stories of spirits and puccas. I told the story of the slootath, a creature that comes with the heavy snow and will eat the limb from a man without him even noticing until he goes to scratch himself and screams. Roisa told the story of the angenga. The angenga are men brought back to life precisely one week from their death to carry out some task for Wealm. Usually it is to deliver a message of love or lust to the latest mortal woman who has caught his eye. Once they have undertaken Wealm's bidding, the god forgets about the angenga and they wander the land, slowly decaying until they cannot walk, only crawl. They never die, the angenga. There are stories of disembodied angenga hands strangling a man in his sleep, and even of a clump of angenga hairs finding their way into someone's throat and choking them. Hilder looks like an angenga newly risen. The wound in his chest, which I can see through the tear in his tunic, is not completely healed. It is red around its edges and looks like it is eager to begin breaking and suppurating. Perhaps the welpa was not enough, its lifelight too dim. Or perhaps he was dead too long.

He stops struggling with his bonds but continues to glare at Casmel with his sallow eyes.

"I am listening," he says.

"Tell Slek Mydra to cease his search. Tell him that dealing with us has not been quite the trouble-free undertaking he doubtless imagined it to be." Casmel points at the sunken corpse of Chayn Syrunn to illustrate his point. "Tell him to go to the Jarl and explain that Alys Clainh is dead. Dead at his hand. The job is done. If he does this, I will see that the Sceada receives a heavy bag of coin before a month has passed. A *heavy* bag. Do you understand?"

"I understand that you have lost your mind," says Hilder, grinning. His gums are pale as the belly of a toad. I don't think he will last long. "Mydra will not be bought. The Sceada are fools for honour and loyalty."

"Everyone can be bought," says Casmel. "Everyone has a price. Everyone has a coin, the weight of which will take them down."

"Not the Sceada. And certainly not Slek Mydra. His loyalty to the Jarl is absolute."

"Just *tell* him," says Casmel.

"For what good it will do, I will tell him. He is still going to gut you."

"Everyone has a price," says Casmel, and turns away from Hilder. "Right," he says to Ethra and me. "Let's get away from this place. It has the stink of death about it."

"That's *him*," says Ethra, pointing at Hilder and pinching her nose. "I thought it was the other one, the dead one, the one that killed me, but it isn't. It's the slaughterman, the one who is pretending to be alive."

"I am *not* pretending," snaps Hilder. "I live. I live, you little gedknot! I live." But there is a thread—no, a thick *rope*—of doubt in his voice.

"If you say so," says Ethra.

We are ready to go in just a few minutes. I am sat behind Casmel on Skep, my arms about his waist, and Ethra is on Lata. Casmel has his mare's rein tucked into his belt.

"You only have to concentrate on not falling off," he says to Ethra.

"I think I can manage that," Ethra replies, but not with any confidence.

As we begin to ride away, Hilder shouts, "Untie me! You can't leave me bound. There are nef here about."

"He has a point," I say, keeping my voice low.

"I considered it," says Casmel. "But I don't think there is any danger of him being taken for a meal. There is something very... *off* about him."

"I think you're right about that. But you're wrong about Slek Mydra. He will not be bought. The Sceada are death-loyal."

"Oh, I know. But if we'd let Hilder live with no purpose, then Mydra would have suspected something was amiss. Maybe not that we are spying on him through the eyes of his lackey, but *something*."

"Of course," I say, then yawn.

"You must stay awake, Alys," says Casmel. "We need to give Mydra time to find Hilder if we are to learn anything."

"But I am *so* tired," I say.

"I know," he says. "But you must keep your eyes open for a little while yet."

"Tell me a story, then," I say.

"Don't we tell stories to help children sleep?" says Casmel. "Isn't that the opposite of what we are trying to achieve here?"

"Stories have never made me sleep," I say. "My mother had to sing me to sleep, or stroke my back, or rub my palm with her thumb. Stories always made me more wakeful. I always wished to know what happen next."

"I have no stories," says Casmel. "Unless you want to hear about the many games of spedig I have won and lost. Or, perhaps, you would like to hear about the time I drank so much ale I tried to saddle a cow, thinking it was Lata?"

"I would not," I say.

"Please yourself," says Casmel. "It is a very funny story and your loss if you do not hear it. Ethra? Do you have a tale?"

"None I want to tell. Unless you would hear the First Story."

"Tell it," I say. I have heard it many times, though often it changes at the edges and becomes interesting again.

She tells it.

In the beginning, there was nothing.

There was no thing and there was no time.

And then arose the Moment.

And being the only thing that was, the Moment was Everything.

And it was Everything all at once.

It was as a roaring, crashing wave, obliterating the nothing in an instant.

But in its violent suddenness, it created, instead of nothing, the shuddering chaos known as the Dwolma.

The Moment sat at the centre of the Dwolma and the Moment was the Dwolma.

And the Moment was afraid and could find no peace.

And so the Moment began to bring order to the chaos, which was the Dwolma, which was the Moment.

It began by creating Heaven.

Heaven was a calmness in the midst of chaos.

But the Moment found the calmness of Heaven only served to accentuate the shuddering chaos beyond its edges.

And so the Moment created distraction within Heaven, things to catch the eye and draw the attention away from the terrifying spectacle of the Dwolma.

The Moment created the Mountains of Eormen, the Meadows of Apay, the Sea of Byre, the Desert of Brunetha, the Forest of Healstor, the Swamps of Merscud, the Valley of Faerseeth, the Frozen Wastes of Frorelm, the Plateau of Lehng.

But it was not enough to distract the Moment from the Dwolma. It was not enough to assuage the Moment's terror.

And so the Moment created the gods: Fryth, Gewith, Seros, Wyrchen, Byradu, Bacotha, Memynd, Beolas and many more besides whose names are forgotten or were never known or were never named.

And to the Moment's delight, the gods, being of the Moment, began their own makings.

They made the skies and the stars. They made our world and, to give it companionship, the moon. And in our world they made all the things that they enjoyed in their Heaven: mountains, meadows, seas, deserts, forests, swamps, valleys, frozen wastes, plateaus.

And then they made the peoples of the world, beginning with Derenderlic and Shiblessi, from whom all peoples were begat.

But soon there were too many people, and they appeared always in conflict with one another, and their conflict was without end because it was of no consequence.

The gods did not know what to do.

But the Moment did.

The Moment created a new god, and that god's name is Wealm, and he is the God of Death. And Wealm created for himself his Fields, between the Mountain of Eormen and the Meadows of Apay, and from that day forward, there was a consequence to conflict and the number of a man's days was given a limit.

Soon, Ethra's voice is just a sound without meaning, a comforting buzz. I try to focus on the words but cannot make a meaning of them.

When the sound stops and the story is done, I say, "Tell it again."

And she tells it, even if I do not hear it.

Somehow, I manage to stay awake for the next three hours. But after that, it is useless trying to resist.

I watch the rat—body fat as a piglet's, tail longer than a grown man's leg—as it burrows its way into Chayn Syrunn's withered corpse. I tug at the cords that bind my wrists, but I haven't the strength to loosen them. For a moment I can't understand what is happening. Have I been betrayed? Has Casmel Durn, the Scur, pulled the wool over my eyes once more?

And then I realise. I am not me. At least I am not in my own body. I am in the skin of Eftas Hilder. It feels wrong this time. It isn't the same as when I saw through my father's eyes or Casmel's eyes. I can feel his skin on me, as if I am wearing it as a garment. And there is a layer of hot grease between it and me. It is a sickening sensation.

I almost withdraw back to wakefulness, but somehow I am able to find the nerve to hold fast.

The rat seems as repulsed by Syrunn's flesh as I am by Hilder's. It scuttles backward from the corpse and hacks up a gobbet of half-chewed... *something*. And then it looks at me. At Hilder. It sniffs the air once and again. Then it takes a few tentative steps toward me before sniffing the air again. It could be my imagination, but there seems to be an expression of disgust on the rat's face. It scampers away. Just in time. A sword blade falls where, a moment before, the beast was sniffing and expressing its distaste.

I recognise the weapon. It has hooks along its blade, designed to drag entrails steaming into the cold air. It is a Sceada's weapon.

Slek Mydra's face lurches before mine.

"What happened here, slaughterman?" he says in his soft, reasonable voice. "Is that... Syrunn?"

"Yes," I say. Hilder says. "Cut me loose."

"Why is he dead and you are strung up like a maiden sacrifice?" The Sceada's nose wrinkles. "And why do you smell so... sour?"

It is a relief when Mydra backs away from me.

"Cut me loose," says Hilder.

"You have not answered my question. Why are you alive while he is... like that?"

"They had a message for you. They let me live to deliver it."

"They?"

"Cut me loose."

"Who are 'they'? Speak."

"The Scur who tricked us with his map, Aryc Clainh's daughter and a girl who... whose skin... came off."

"Another Glyster?"

"I do not know. The Scur claimed it was Alys Clainh's doing, this... skinning. He said she would do it to us, too. He said there were spores, that... Or something. I can't remember. It was confusing."

"He tricked you, that is what you are saying, no?"

"No. I don't know. Possibly. Cut me loose."

"And what was this message?"

"He said that you should not follow him. He said that you should go back to Gafol and tell the Jarl that you took care of Clainh's kin. He said that within the month you would receive a heavy bag of coin. He said—"

"He said!" the Sceada roars.

His sword blurs toward me... and buries itself in the trunk above my head. I feel the whole tree tremble violently. It is a wonder I don't snap into wakefulness.

"He mocks me, this Scur," says Mydra, his voice low once more. "Twice now, he has mocked me. The first time, he mocked my intelligence with that deceptive map of his. And now... now he mocks my loyalty, he mocks my honour. He tells me to deceive the Jarl, the Jarl who is as my own brother, who calls *me* brother." He reaches over my head and wrenches his sword from the tree. "I will gut him. I will gut him in the Old Way, so he will live and see and *feel* while I make a noose from his innards and hang him from a witchtree."

It is said that those who hang from a witchtree cannot go to the Fields of Wealm. Given what I have heard of Wealm recently, that may not be a bad thing.

"And then," the Sceada continues, "I will drag the Glystgedder to Gafol and I will make her kneel before her father and I will make her watch as I gut *him* in the Old Way."

Chapter 24

The Eeffenn Sea

The forest thins, and within the hour, we are riding on scrub. We put a ridge between our group and the Fisher Road, but occasionally we hear travellers—cartwheels, hoofs, voices. My leg is starting to ache, every jolt from the uneven ground reminding me of Syrunn with his sword to my throat, twisting the arrow, then twisting it again.

The air begins to cool, to thin as the forest did, and soon I can smell the sea. I am reminded of days spent at Brim, collecting shells with my mother, fishing for crab with my father, of the time I got stung by a tide jelly and my father made a poultice of various weeds that clung to nearby rocks.

Wherever there is a thing that will hurt us, there is usually a thing that will heal. You just have to look around. When you are in pain, look closest for a salve; there is no need for wandering and looking at horizons.

But what if you have no choice but to wander? What if the thing you need is very far away?

A gull shrieks overhead, then another. Soon, a whole squabble of them.

"There," says Casmel, pointing. "Leax."

I lean out so I can see past him.

Clusters of steep and pointed tiled roofs sweep down to the glittering sheet of the sea. The water is dotted with so many boats it is a wonder they are not crashing into one another.

"We will stop here," says Casmel. "I will go into town, find out what I can about Utlath. Purchase a map, perhaps. And while I'm there get a stronger balm for your wound. I have heard you hissing through your teeth this last two hours."

I thought I had concealed my pain well. Clearly not.

"Get us some cooked fish while you are there," says Ethra. "It has been too long since I have eaten well. And this will be my last meal as a Glyster."

"Very well, Ethra," says Casmel, smiling. "Cooked fish."

I resist the urge to tell Ethra that this may well be the last meal any of us eat, as Glyster or otherwise. We know nothing of the Dead City or what dangers it might hold. I know only that it scared El enough that she did not dare enter its walls.

We find a patch of dry ground, Ethra and I, and sit wrapped in our cloaks. There is a wind from the Eeffenn Sea, salty and cool.

"What will you do when you are free of the Glyst?" I ask.

221

"Pull at my skin a while, just to be sure," says Ethra. "Then… I don't know. I would stay with you and Cass. Or with you and El. I would help with the work. But I would do so as myself, as I was before, when I was not something from a nightmare."

"You are not a nightmare, Ethra. Your Glyst would be useful to the Harbour. You can be in two places at once. We might not have survived that ambush if not for your gift."

"Do not call it that," says Ethra. "Please. And we would not have been there *to be* ambushed if it were not for my Glyst."

"It was your wish to be rid of it that put us in harm's way," I say, and regret it immediately. It was a mean remark.

"I know," says Ethra. "And I am sorry. I am sorry for *all* the harm I have caused. My mammy and daddy… they…" She looks out to sea. "They tried to hide me. The Jarl of Mella… had them killed. Hung upside down and bled-out. Like pigs. That is what he said they were for risking the lives of every man, woman and child of Mella. Pigs. Or worse: foorstig."

I am visited by a memory of myself strung up like a pig, like a foorstig, bleeding into the Seven Cups. And, as with every time I recall that experience, it is as if it happened so recently I expect to feel the pain and the itch from the slow-healing wounds, and my heart drums so hard it is like it is trying to escape the prison of my chest.

"I should have run as soon as my Glyst showed itself," says Ethra. "Instead I begged my mammy and daddy to hide me. I was so afraid."

"Of course you were. You were just a child. You *are* just a child."

"I know. But I should have run. Everybody would have thought I was taken by an animal. I was always playing in the woods. I was always careless. My Glyst could have been my burden to bear and not the reason for my parents' deaths. I should have run. And I did. Once I heard that the Jarl had sent word to Feeshun that my blood was for sale. I ran, but too late."

"You can't blame yourself, Ethra. Fear is a terrible thing. It makes us feel like running and nails our feet to the ground at the same time."

"When it first happened, I thought it was a nightmare and that I would awaken at any moment to the smell of honeyed oatcakes and the sound of my parents talking about the day ahead, their tasks and the prospect of rest at day's end, that I would hear them kiss and she would call him her scappwud, which is an old Mella word for 'sweet apple tree'. But I didn't smell honeyed oatcakes or hear my mammy call my daddy her scappwud, because it wasn't a nightmare. It was happening. There were two of me, staring at each other. And I could see through both pairs of eyes at once. One me was nothing but skin, the other had no skin at all. One looked like the work of a butcher, the other the work of a tanner. I screamed. Both of me screamed. My daddy almost killed me. He thought I was some monstrosity come to kill his daughter. He thought I was one of the Byreghan come down from the Beorstehd Mountains to eat flesh and lay its eggs that beget more Byreghan. It was only when I cried out "Daddy!" that he stayed his axe. For a minute, they just stared. And then my mammy came to the skin-me and held me, and my daddy took the body-me in his arms, and they both rocked me, body and skin, until I was asleep. When I awoke, I was whole-me again and was almost able to convince myself it had all been a dream. But, the next day, a trader came, looking for cider to exchange for tools and pots. He had a grefa stone on a string around his neck, this man, and it began whistling. And that was that." She turns away from the sea and looks at me. There are tears in her eyes. "I would be rid of it. This gift."

"Aye." I squeeze her hand.

"Tell me something," says Ethra.

"What?"

"Anything," she says. Then, "No, not anything. Something important. About you. Tell me something that hurts you the way the Glyst hurts me. Let me feel that I am not alone in my pain."

"Very well."

I tell her of the Ritual of the Seven Cuts and the Seven Cups, and then we sit and watch the boats bobbing on the Eeffenn Sea and listen to the gulls crying overhead, and do not speak until Casmel returns.

As promised, he has brought cooked fish and a poultice.

We eat the fish with relish, and then Ethra changes my dressing and applies the new poultice. I catch Casmel watching as Ethra applies the pulped herbs to my thigh.

"I think she can manage unsupervised," I say, raising an eyebrow at him.

"Just wanted to make sure she was doing it right," he says, turning away quickly. But not so quickly I don't see the red in his cheeks.

"I couldn't get a map," he says. "Of Utlath. The locals get quite testy when you even mention the place. The only thing I managed to find out was that the Hollow, the Glystleeches, are to be found at the old docks of the city or thereabouts. Everyone I spoke to advised against it. Those who go too far into the city do not often come back. The best materials for making grefa stones are to be found in the middle of the city, but those from the buildings just a hundred yards in will do."

I am too tired to catch his inference. With a bellyful of fish and the pain in my leg at last abated, I am asleep in no time.

Slek Mydra stares at me.

"You look terrible," he says. "Your skin is like a bogtoad's belly and you smell like... I do not know what you smell like."

"I do not want to die," I say. No. *Eftas Hilder* says. "I am afraid."

"Afraid?" says Mydra, his tone mocking. He looks at me, at Hilder, with naked pity. "So what? So what if you are afraid? You think I am never afraid? That I do not experience fear? It matters not. Fear and courage are the same river. When you are afraid, you are swimming against the current. When you are brave, you are swimming *with* the current, letting it take you where it will. Either way, you are in the river. And the river can bring pain, suffering, death. But it is easier to swim with the current. Once you realise this and embrace the fear, accept that it is simply... *there*, you have the makings of a warrior. It is not the fear that paralyses. It is the battling of it. So say we Sceada, anyway."

He stands and walks across the clearing in which they appear to have made camp. They are surrounded by oaks. For the remainder of our journey, we did not see any oak. I wonder where they are.

"I do not want to die," says Eftas. His voice is as quiet as Mydra's but without the stone and iron.

He looks down at his hands. They look bloodless and wet, soft, as if they could be cut open with a wooden spoon.

He looks at Mydra, opens his mouth to speak.

And then everything turns grey, and Mydra is gone.

He looks at his hands again. They are grey, too. Not the bloodless grey of a moment ago, but a dry, dusty grey. And then I see the hundreds of tiny mushrooms that are sprouting from his skin.

"I am dead," he says. "I am dead again."

He tries to stand but hasn't the strength and slumps back against the tree behind him.

"Mydra?" he tries to shout, but only whispers. "Mydra?"

Something is coming toward him from the grey woods.

It is not Slek Mydra.

It is a man of sorts. If a man were made of sticky, steaming rope and had no face, only a hole where a face should be.

The hole speaks.

"It is coming," says the hole. "The Gravene."

Chapter 25

The Gates of Utlath

"What?" says Casmel. "Was it Mydra?"

I can still smell and taste the dryness, the greyness of that other place.

I sit up. Casmel and Ethra are staring at me impatiently.

"Was it?" says Ethra.

"Yes."

"Where were they?"

"I don't know. I didn't recognise it from our route."

"Maybe they've lost our trail," says Casmel.

"Maybe the Sceada has decided to take you up on your offer, Cass," says Ethra.

I shake my head.

"He would not," I say. "It is not in the nature of the Sceada. But Casmel could be right. With Syrunn gone, they would have had a harder task of following us."

"I give thanks to Gewith if that is so," says Casmel.

"Luck," I say, more to myself than anything, "is a bucket with a hole."

I notice then that the sun is creeping over the horizon, turning the sea to molten metal. Already, there are boats out there on the water, just little silhouettes. There are only a few gulls and they are mostly silent. Against the quiet, I can hear the waves and the occasional call of a fisherman as he hauls in his net. It is peaceful, calming. I let it soak into me, as bread soaks in a strengthening broth. I suspect it is the last peace I will know, that we will know, for quite some time to come. I find myself thinking of Dwynan Furral, the boy I kissed more than a year ago, behind the Jarl's stable, during the Festival of Seros, and how his lips were soft and tasted of yellowberries. He had always spoken—when we spoke, before that kiss silenced him on all subjects—of his dream to build a boat and live the life of a simple fisherman, working the waters at Brim and along the west coast.

"We'd best get going," says Casmel, placing a hand on my arm. "How's the leg?"

I give it a little flex. It aches, but not nearly as much as it had before the application of last night's poultice.

"Not too bad," I say. "Thank you. For the balm and for coming with us to Utlath."

He just nods, stands and begins gathering up the camp.

We are riding before the sun has freed itself of the horizon. I am back on Skep now, and Ethra is riding with Casmel. For some reason, I thought to tell Casmel that my leg wasn't quite up to the ride and I would sit with him, but then I felt silly, said nothing and just climbed onto my own mare. We cross the Fisher Road then cut across scrubland until we are on the Coast Road, about a mile south of Leax. It is an uphill ride with a brisk wind off the Eeffenn Sea, and we do not speak for several hours. We do not speak until we see the city of Utlath, the Dead City, begin to rise, seemingly from the ground like some vast and outlandish tree ahead of us.

Its three towers come into view first, spiralled round one another, just like on the map El had shown us the morning we set off on our journey. How the city's architects succeeded in twisting the huge, white stones from which the tower is made, I cannot imagine. Until I remember that this is a city made by Glysters, a place so drenched in the Glyst that the smallest stone chipped from its walls and drilled with a hole will cry out when it senses the presence of a Glyster.

As the city rises, smaller towers begin to join the central trinity. Some of these are twisted about one another, too. Some taper to needle-like points, some are domed, others are fatter at the top than the bottom, like mushrooms. Some have so many windows it is a wonder they do not collapse as they are more nothing than something. Some have no windows at all. There is an intricate network of walkways between towers. Trees grow from some roofs, and the walls of many of the towers are cracked and ivy-laced.

The walls loom into view next. They circle the city, but not evenly as I'd imagined. Their path is snaking, undulating and miles long. They are made of the same white blocks as the towers, but each block is colossal. Here and there, stones are missing. The gaps left behind could contain our roundhouse, or possibly even the Jarl's squarehouse. Some stones are carved with the faces of men and women: old, young, beautiful, grotesque. There are steps zigzagging down to each carving from the crenellated top of the wall. For maintenance, I assume.

The Coast Road reaches its zenith before steeply sloping down toward the city. From here we can see the moat that surrounds the city, fed by the nearby Eeffen Sea, and we can see the Gates of Utlath.

The Gates of Utlath, closed tight, are made from the wood of trees that would have to be three-hundred-feet high and a hundred-feet wide at breast height. But the gates themselves are not what cause me to cry out—and cry out I do, unable to help myself—it is what stands at one side of the gate that has this effect. And not just on me. Casmel and Ethra both make sounds of shock and wonder.

On one side of the gate, carved into the stone, is a wolf. Its mouth is open wide, revealing ferocious teeth and a lolling tongue. Its mane is thick, and its body and limbs strain with muscle. On the other side of the gate is a woman. She is cloaked, carries a bow, nocked, anchored and ready to loose. There is a sword at her belt, and a shield and spear on her back. Her face wears an expression that could be rage or determination, or perhaps even madness. What is most extraordinary about that face is that it is *mine*.

"She stands at the Gates of Utlath," I say to myself.

I remember a song by this name from my childhood. That is, I remember the title and the melody—haunting and rousing—but not all the words. In fact, I can remember only three lines:

She stands at the Gates of Utlath, her finewolf at her side

She dies at the Gates of Utlath, her finewolf at her side

And forever more and ever after, every Glyster cried.

"Alys," says Ethra, her voice so wispy, I have to check she has not separated into skin and body. She hasn't. "It's you. It's lucky we're sat on horseback and not standing, or we would all fall down."

"It can't be," I say, even though I am looking directly at my own gargantuan likeness.

"It is," says Casmel. "It's you. But bigger. A lot bigger." And then he just switches his gaze back and forth between me and the statue, his mouth hanging slack.

"Straggis wasps will build a nest on your tongue if you do not close your mouth," I say. Then, "It must be a coincidence. It *must* be."

"Yes," says Casmel. "Must be." But he doesn't sound convinced. "But if it isn't… what does it mean?"

"It doesn't mean anything. It's a coincidence. Someone who looks like me. That's all."

"Someone who looks like you," says Casmel. "I mean that makes more sense than… well… this." Again, he sounds doubtful. "She has more muscle than you, for one thing."

He's right. She looks powerful, this huge, stone… effigy?

I dismiss the word quickly. Effigy? Ridiculous. And yet…

"Are they scars?" asks Ethra. "Or was the statue damaged when the Cwalee came?"

There are, indeed, scars: on the cheeks, the forehead, the temple, across the bridge of the nose, on the hands and arms. They have the look of battle scars: random.

But there are two scars which do not look like battle scars, which do not look random. These scars make me feel so dizzy I grip Skep's reins with the tightness of a novice rider. These scars are to each of the wrists of the statue.

They are my scars.

They are the second and third scars of the Ritual of the Seven Cuts and the Seven Cups.

I take a deep breath, then another, pushing the dizziness out of my head.

There will be an explanation for all of this, I tell myself. And it will be a sensible one that makes me feel foolish, and I will laugh whenever I hear the word 'effigy' again.

"Let's get this done," I say, trying to put a note of dismissiveness in my voice. If I can convince Casmel and Ethra that this is nothing but happenstance, a statue of a woman who *just happens* to look like me, maybe I can begin to convince myself.

As we ride the sloping road down toward the gates of the Dead City, I deliberately keep my eyes fixed on the ground ahead of me. I do not want to see that statue, that likeness, growing as I near it. I only look at it when we are so close I am looking at it from beneath, from an angle I have never seen myself before.

"Is my nose really that big?" I ask.

"None of you is that big," says Casmel.

"You know what I mean."

"No, your nose is not big. It is a very dainty nose. It is the nose of a princess."

"Don't overcook the stew," I say, an old Gafol turn. "We did not ask for soup."

"Sorry," says Casmel, grinning. "What I meant to say was your nose is perfectly adequate. It is an unremarkable nose. And certainly not as big as the nose of a colossal statue."

"Fool," I say and roll my eyes at him. Then I look to see if there is a way into the city.

The moat is about ten yards across, and there is a wide bridge continuing from the edge of the road to the gate. But the wall around the closed gate is solid. There are holes in the wall off to the right, about thirty yards along, but no way over the moat to take advantage of them. We could ride around the perimeter of the city, but it would take a good hour or more, with no guarantee of finding a way in.

"Didn't the people in Leax suggest a small boat?" I say. "A coracle, perhaps?"

"No," says Casmel, sighing. "They were very unhelpful. Perhaps, they thought it was for our own good to be so… uninstructive."

"I'm not going back," says Ethra. "If that's what you're thinking."

"Nobody's thinking that," I say. I look up at the statue of my likeness. "Then we have to climb. And that is the only thing with handholds enough."

"I am not good with heights," says Casmel.

"Then don't look down," says Ethra. "Or you can stay here."

"That isn't an option," says Casmel.

We take the horses downslope toward the coast and secure them in a copse of spindly trees that look to be made more of salt than wood. If they are of a mind to wander, there is little stopping them. And they can probably be seen from the road by anyone with more than a passing interest. But we don't have many options. Or any options, for that matter. We have to act quickly. We have no notion of how far behind us Mydra is, and there is no entertaining the notion he has headed back to Gafol to await Casmel's promise of coin. It is true he seemed to have lost our trail, but there is no telling how quickly he might have picked it up again.

I step on the toe of my own giant boot and, finding purchase on the 'leather' leg-windings, begin my slow, strenuous ascent. First me, then Ethra, then Casmel.

The wind picks up from Eeffenn Sea. It comes in chill, wet gusts, shoving at us. Twice, we have to stop and hold tight until the worst of it is over. On both occasions, I hear Casmel praying to Lyfbyre, the God of the Four Winds.

I have almost reached my own vast shoulder when I hear a sharp intake of breath from Ethra. I look down and see her leaning back, her hands scrabbling at nothing. I try to reach for her.

But she is falling.

And then another gust bullies me from the east. I lose my own grip, and I am falling too.

Chapter 26

Battle Scars

Somehow I am falling faster than Ethra, or so it seems, because I pass her, as if I am eager to strike the ground first.

And then I am yanked upwards, hands gripping my shoulders.

I look up.

It is Ethra. She is carrying me. And she is flying.

Not Skin-Ethra, not billowing-sail-Ethra, but Whole-Ethra. Ethra-Ethra.

I look down and see Casmel staring up at me, his mouth hanging open for the second time this morning.

Ethra lowers me onto a walkway on top of the city wall. A moment later she returns with Casmel, whose mouth is still hanging open.

"I didn't know you could do that," I say. My heart is still galloping in my chest and my voice is tremulous.

"Nor did I," says Ethra, smiling. "It's like my skin is flying, but it is carrying the rest of me inside it."

"And how did you carry us?" asks Casmel. "There is little muscle on you."

"I don't know," says Ethra. "I just felt… strong. I think, when I am flying, I could carry you both if I wanted to. One in each hand."

"That's good to know," says Casmel. "Because it might be a while before my legs are working again, and that is a lot of stairs." He points to the steps carved into the inner wall that zigzag to the ground beneath us.

"I could carry you, if you'd like," says Ethra.

Casmel considers it then shakes his head. "I would get used it and soon we will not be able to call upon this talent."

"True enough," says Ethra.

We all walk down the stairs.

While the taller buildings and towers we pass on our descent are made of the same white blocks as the city wall, the two- and thee-storey buildings which cluster around them and edge the wide streets are made of ordinary stone and timber. They have fallen into considerable disrepair, in some cases collapsing entirely. Here and there among the ruins, I see skulls and bones. On top of the heap that one building has become, a wooden doll, warped by damp, stares at me with bulging eyes. It is dark down here in the shadows of the towers and will remain so until the sun is overhead some hours from now.

I step onto the main road through the city—its stones are loose, the surface uneven and potholed—and then I notice the gates and laugh.

They are rotted and split, with fissures easily big enough for a man to walk through. They are not the imposing barrier we encountered on the other side of the wall.

"Some Glyst?" says Casmel.

"I assume so," I say.

"I did not think a Glyst could last so long," says Ethra.

It makes me wonder what other Glysts are out there in the world, lingering. Are there things that we think of as commonplace, which are in fact old, enduring Glysts? A certain tree or lake or mountain?

I start down the road. It leads in a straight line directly to the central towers, which I estimate to be at least two miles away. We will need to turn left at some point, head east toward the coast, but there are no such turnings yet. We are crowded in by buildings and the remnants of buildings. I get the sense—distinct and emphatic—that we are being watched from those properties that might hide someone or something. Worse, I get the sense that we are being watched from the fallen structures that couldn't conceivably hide anything larger than a welpa.

We have been walking for some ten minutes with still no turning in sight, when Casmel stops and says in a quiet voice, a shamed voice, "I'll go no further."

"What?" I ask, certain that I have misheard him or that there might be some meaning to his words I am failing to grasp.

He points to a statue that appears to have fallen from the sky, crushing two wooden buildings. It looks like it might have been a woman at some stage. It is not only the fall that has rendered it difficult to identify but the fact that the white stone from which it was carved has been chiselled mercilessly so it is a featureless thing, pocked and scarred. It would be easy to believe that it is a statue of Bacotha, the God of Disease and brother of Memynd, God of Madness. But I know that is not the case. This statue, whoever it represented, has been plundered for grefa stones.

"I will get all I need here," he says.

"What?" I say again, but I know perfectly his meaning now.

"I cannot risk death," he says.

"I had not taken you for a coward, Casmel," I say.

"That is because I am *not* a coward," he says, face flushed with anger, jaw clenched. "You have *seen* that I am not a coward."

I think of how he faced down Slek Mydra across the spedig table. I think of how he followed on foot through nef-haunted forests. I think of how he bluffed Hilder and Syrunn with an arrow aimed at his chest. And I know he is not a coward and I am being unfair. But that knowledge does not abate my anger, my sense of betrayal, and it does not keep those things from showing in my voice.

"So why have you risked so much thus far?" I demand.

"For this," he says, pointing at the disfigured statue. "The stones." He begins rummaging through his bag, refusing to meet my eye.

"Stones?" I say. "By which you mean 'coin', of course. Your beloved coin."

"Yes, coin," he replies, pulling a small hammer and chisel from his bag. He must have purchased them in Awlen or Leax. "But I have no love of it."

"Gedmouth! It is all you think about. I foolishly believed you were genuine in your desire to accompany us here, to help us. What an idiot. There are scabwolves whose brains are less eaten-at than mine. And the funny thing is, you didn't need us, not really. This far in, there are no dangers it would seem. Only the climb itself." I point back toward the gate. "And that was an unnecessary risk. You never needed us at all. I doubt you have ever needed anyone in your entire, stupid, selfish life."

"I was a slave," he says. "For most of my life."

"A slave to what?" I ask, thinking he is speaking in allusions. "A slave to money. A slave to the thrill of spedig?"

"A slave," he says, his voice flat. He speaks the word as if he does not wish to invest it with too much meaning, as if he really doesn't want to speak it at all. "Just a slave." His arms hang limp, the hammer in one hand, the chisel in the other.

"What?"

"When my father came back from the Battle of Thelland, he was changed. He was a good man before he went away, a terrible one when he returned. He was afraid and weak and angry. He drank and he gambled and made a debt so large it could not be repaid. And so he was taken before the Orl, who is like your Jarl. The Orl sold him to repay the debt. He sold him, my mother, my brother and me. I was eight years old. Me and my father were sold to a farmer in a neighbouring town, a place called Tilbur. My brother, a year younger than me, was sold to a trader from Besniwehn, an island far to the north of Abegan, where there is always snow and ice. My mother was sold to a Leccan as his wife."

His jaw clenches, and I do not know if it is rage or an attempt to stifle tears. Perhaps it is both.

"Nine years I was a slave," he says. "It felt ten times that. The farmer who owned us, Gullen, treated us as less than cattle. Far less."

"Those marks you said were battle scars…" I say.

"They were not battle scars. The lash. It was used often. More so on my father because the drink had weakened him and he was not as useful a tool. But the wounds inflicted on my father weakened him further, inviting the lash all the more."

I remember the curious piece of knotted leather I found in his bag and how he had been angered when I handled it. A piece of knotted leather. As of the end of a lash. He must have kept it as a reminder of who he was, *what* he was.

He crouches next to the statue and chisels a chunk of stone from it.

"Gullen lost me in a game of spedig to a trader from one of the desert places in the south. But the trader said his people did not keep slaves, and he freed me. I asked if he would play on to free my father, but he told me that a father is a son's responsibility. Gullen, eager to replace his lost coin, said he would sell my father to me, and he named a high price. He laughed when he set his price, saying my father was not worth more than a toenail. But he swore it, that price. He swore it in front of many people, and so he must honour it. I asked the trader who freed me if he would lend me enough coin to begin making my own, and he did. One day I will go to those Southlands, maybe even live there. The people seem so much finer than those of Abegan."

He chips another stone from the statue, inspects it, and sets it aside.

"I grew my coin by playing spedig, and playing it well. For the most part. But every time I had nearly enough to free my father, I would lose, and I would lose heavily. I never fell much into debt, but I could never acquire enough to pay Gullen's fee. Coin is a funny thing. It seems real when it is sitting in your hand, even more so when you have a purse full of it. But it can vanish so easily, so mysteriously, like early morning mist when the sun touches it."

He chips another stone, but this one is too small to have a hole drilled in it and he tosses it away.

"My father will not live long. The punishments meted out by Gullen and the punishments he inflicted upon himself with drink will finish him soon."

He looks at me. His eyes gleam with the threat of tears, but he doesn't cry.

"I will not have him die a slave. I will not have the good man he was be thrown into a shallow hole in sour ground along with the bad man he became.

I will free him and I will give him the warrior's ending that he deserves. Because that good man who went to war is still within my father. And if I die, there is nobody who will give him that."

I nod. It is all I can do. There are no words. Or I cannot think of them.

"Good luck," says Ethra. "Good luck, Casmel Durn."

I nod.

Casmel nods.

He goes back to his chiselling, and Ethra and I continue up the road.

And suddenly I think of the words.

I turn and say, loud enough that I hope he hears me, "They *were* battle scars, Cass. They were."

Chapter 27

A Familiar Glyst

Eventually, perhaps a mile from the three coiling towers, the road branches off. Not just east, but west, northeast and northwest.

We head east. There is more ruin on display on the eastward road. Few of the buildings are standing, and those that are sag as if rotten at the very core. One structure, possibly a chandler during Utlath's heyday—there is a carving of a candle above the door—looks as if a single kick would cause it to collapse in a wet heap. Another—a butcher's shop given the hooks on display—has a bloated quality, like the ripe ball mushrooms Roisa and I would kick. If I were to poke the outer skin of that abandoned establishment with the point of my sword, it might burst. Or it might deflate in an instant, becoming a small, wrinkled thing.

The whole street smells of rot, and not the natural rot of, say, the forest floor or a dead tree. It is the rot of sickness. It is as the rot that took my mother.

"It's funny how alike you and Cass are," says Ethra.

"You are talking for talking's sake now," I say. "Because the silence frightens you."

"That is, indeed, true," says Ethra. "My bladder and bowels are competing for my attention, and my heart is like a straggis wasp caught in a copper pot. It is also true, however, that you and Cass are very alike."

"Talk if you must," I say, feigning disinterest.

"Well, you are both about the same age. He, a little older. But not much. You are both the same height. He is handsome and you are pretty."

"There's more to people than how they look, Ethra."

"I had not finished. You have scars and he has scars. Yours from the Ritual of the Seven Cuts and the Seven Cups. He, from his time as a bondsman."

"A slave," I say.

"I was taught that 'slave' was an impolite word."

"It is. But it is also an honest word. Some things should not be permitted to hide behind a fine cloak or a bouquet of herbs."

"He lost his mother. You lost your mother. You are trying to save your father and he is trying to save his father."

"I think it is too late for him to save his father. I think he just hopes to give him back his dignity for a time. A brief time."

"And that is a good thing. Cass is a good person, for all his air of roguery. And you are alike in that manner, too. Cass is a good person, and you are a good person. And you, Alys, are a…" Her nose wrinkles. "*Horrible!*"

"I'm sorry…"

"That smell…"

It hits me a fraction of a second later. And it is horrible. It is as if the rank stink of the entire street has suddenly concentrated itself into our immediate vicinity. It is a smell so awful it should be visible. There should be a noxious cloud of acid greens and burning yellows curling about us. I stop in my tracks then turn on the spot, trying to locate the source of the appalling stench.

A rat.

Except it is the size of a horse.

Its bones thread in and out of its hairless flesh. Its head is disproportionately long and its mouth—opening now, wider and wider—has not the incisors of a rodent but rows upon rows of what must be hundreds of yellow thorn-like teeth that look like they could shred the meat from the bone in seconds. Its eyes are blood-red and bulging. It has arms that seem almost of human design, but they end in long, razor-sharp, curving talons, like that of the Great Eagle.

It rears up on its hind legs and lets out a deep, rumbling hiss, as if it has a belly full of snakes. It swipes at me with one of its talons. I leap back and draw my sword. Its tail, coiled away out of sight until this moment, lashes out and strikes Ethra in the side. She is lifted into the air and lands some yards away with a grunt.

Its other talon comes at me, and I meet it with my blade. The rat pulls back its claw, letting out a hiss of rage and pain. I cannot see that I did much more that score it though, and I am lucky to still have my sword in my hand; the jolt was considerable. I glance over at Ethra. She isn't moving.

This is not a creature I can defeat. But I cannot leave Ethra where she lies.

"Ethra! You need to get up. We need to run!"

The thing's tail is lashing at me, then. Again, I meet it with my sword. And this time, my sword *is* jolted from my hand and doesn't so much as mark the creature's leathery appendage.

I follow my sword as it skitters across the road and manage to pick it up, turn and block one then another swipe from respective talons. Each parry sends jarring pain through my hand, wrist and elbow. I wish I had the muscle of the statue at the gates. I don't think I can keep hold of my sword much longer, so I swap to my left hand. The creature's head darts at me, mouth snapping. I jab its face but strike one of those outer bones, and it is like jabbing at plate armour. The tail sweeps again, aiming for my feet, to trip me, and I jump, as if I am a little girl in Gafol, skipping rope. Its face darts at me again and I jab it once more, this time striking flesh. Either I have struck an already-infected wound or the creature's blood is a poisonous-looking yellow.

I begin to feel dizzy and realise I am holding my breath. If its teeth, tail and talons do not undo me, its odour will. In the name of Beolas, God of Wild Flowers and Herbs, it *stinks*!

The tail comes at me again. I do not attempt to parry it. I attempt, instead, to shuffle back, out of its reach, and am only just successful. I feel the wind from the tip of its tail as it passes an inch from my face.

And then I feel the press of stone against my spine and realise I have backed into a wall and have nowhere to run.

I chance a look over my shoulder and see the cracked and damp-bloated wall of a building. To my left, a closed door with a carving above it so deformed it might be a spray of flowers or a display of offal. It could be the door to the premises of a flower-seller or a haruspex. I lurch for the door. Just in time. The rat's tail smashes into the wall where I was standing with a resounding crack that would have been my bones had I delayed by even a second. I shoulder-barge the door—hoping, praying that my bucket of luck is not dry yet—and it flies in. Momentum carries me forwards and I collide with a table piled with pots and jars. I lose my sword amid the wreckage I have just created. In the gloom, I can't locate it.

And don't have time. The rat thrusts its head through the doorway, snapping inches from my face, and I thank Gewith for the dregs he has left me because the beast is too wide to fit bodily through the doorway. It strains to reach me but cannot. But already the wall around the door is beginning to crack and bulge. It won't hold for more than a few seconds. I pull out my dagger, and when the rat snaps at me again, I dodge and bring myself alongside the thing's head, and thrust my blade into its eye. There is a wet pop and the creature shrieks, pulling back and wrenching itself free of the doorway, my knife still in its leaking socket.

I watch it flee.

Only it doesn't flee. An ordinary animal suffering such an injury would flee, would go back to its den and lick its wounds. But this isn't an ordinary animal. It is doubtless Glystborne. Or if not Glystborne, altered by the Glyst. Instead of fleeing, it bounds toward easier prey.

Ethra.

I unshoulder my bow, reach for an arrow, but even as I do so, I know it is too late. I will never nock and loose the thing before the beast reaches Ethra, and even if I did, it will take five, ten arrows to bring the rat down. I think of those teeth, like thorns, hundreds and hundreds of them, designed for shredding.

"Ethra!"

She does not stir.

And then she is concealed from view by the rat's bulk.

"Ethra!"

The rat rears up.

And somehow I *do* manage to loose an arrow. It strikes the back of the creature's neck. But it doesn't even seem to notice the injury, doesn't so much as swat at it as you would a biting midge. I reach for another arrow. The rat raises one talon, poised to plunge down into Ethra's inert, defenceless form.

"Ethra!"

And then the rat is shrieking again, shrieking as it did when I plunged the blade into its eye.

It is shrieking because, suddenly and for no visible reason, the rat is on fire.

From a space between two crumbling buildings, a man emerges. His hands are gloved in flame. He makes a gesture in the air, as if he is drawing some elaborate character or glyph. I glimpse the hanging afterglow of his burning fingers.

The flames that engulf the rat increase in their intensity. The creature staggers back, away from Ethra, its shrieking becoming a bubbling. It is beginning to cook. Even from where I am, some yards away, the stench is beyond appalling, and I gag repeatedly. The man with burning hands is unperturbed and moves forward with graceful confidence, continuing to inscribe the air—warped now by the heat—with complex characters.

The rat turns to run, but the heat is shrinking its muscles, melting its ligaments. It falls on its side, burning tail lashing violently, almost—but not quite, thankfully—finding motionless Ethra. The rat judders, spasms, then curls in on itself and is still.

The man claps his hands, and the flames go out in an instant. All the flames: those on his hands and those that were engulfing the now-dead rat. He goes to Ethra and kneels down next to her. I grab my sword, sheath it, then nock an arrow and stride out through the doorway and into the street.

"Don't touch her!" I say.

He has saved her, true, but I do not know him and have no reason to trust that his intentions are good.

"My arrow has your heart in its sights," I say.

"I'm sure it does," says the man, his attention still on Ethra. "But you have just seen what I've done to that Glystfell. You would burn quicker."

As if to underscore his threat, there is a loud crack from the rat and its torso collapses in a flurry of embers.

"Glystfell?" I say.

"The rat. There is wild Glyst hereabouts. It changes things. Often not for the better. It can be like a scabwolf's corpse in a well, wild Glyst. A kind of poison. Only it changes more than it kills. But it kills, too."

He puts a hand to Ethra's throat.

"I'm warning you," I say, and close some of the distance between us. The heat from the burning rat is harsh against my face, but the smell is rapidly diminishing in strength and offensiveness. The man is about my father's age. His hair is grey and long, tied in a ponytail. He is wearing a motley combination of colourful robes and trousers and mismatched boots. He has the build of a warrior, though he appears to have no weapons, and there are scars crisscrossing his face that have the irregular appearance of those received in combat.

"If I meant you harm, you'd both be ashes by now. I've been watching you since you descended the wall. You and the idiot scavenger, looking for his traitorstones. Your friend, here, is concussed.

Nothing serious. Her heartbeat is steady. I have herbs that will rouse her back at the Library. We should get her there quickly, though. What's your name?"

"It's none of your business. What's yours?"

"Madec. Madec Teeg."

Chapter 28

Stories and Songs

It takes me a second to identify just why that name seems so familiar.

Madec Teeg.

Then it comes to me in El's matter-of-fact tones:

I saw him on the edge of the Freewood. I was a little younger than you… He was making a fire… instead of using tinder and flint, he just… clicked his fingers… And suddenly his hand was gloved in flame. He held his fingers to the kindling until it was burning steadily.

Then I hear my father:

I'll tell them we saw someone in the Freewood, a man. A man making fire with his bare hands. A man with the Glyst.

Then El once more:

His name was Madec Teeg. He'd had the Glyst for three years and had been chased from his village near the Leccan Forest. His story shamed me because we had not chased Glysters from our village. We had slain them. Five in my lifetime.

"I know you," I say. "I know you, Madec Teeg."

He looks at me with suspicion.

"How?" he says. "You seem too young to have heard of my exploits."

"I don't know of any exploits. Only that you fled your Leccan village when you were about my age and you were briefly looked after by Elsam Clainh, my aunt."

His brow furrows. Then he stands, smiling.

"El?" he says. "El from Gafol?"

"Yes," I say. "She spoke of you."

"That was such a long time ago. But I have not forgotten her. I would be dead without her, I don't doubt."

"And yet you left without a word."

"My Glyst began to go wild. I could feel it slipping from my control. I feared I would hurt her."

I lower my bow but keep the arrow in place.

"And yet she was hurt. I saw it in her eyes."

"I am sorry for that. I wanted to go back, but first I made my way here, to Utlath as was. I had heard of the Hollow, of how they would drain the power from a Glyster."

"And you've been here ever since?"

"I did not arrive here for many years. En route, I was captured by a mercenary named Hytir. He was from the East Edge Islands. The people there did not believe the Cwalee would return, and so they put Glysters to work, treating them as less than people, keeping their numbers low and employing them as useful tools. This was before Bansowa became the ruler of the East Edge. Before the Uprising... and what followed. The Slaughter. I was pressed into service as a weapon. I fought in many battles, none of which I wanted any part of or, more often than not, could even understand the purpose of. After many years, during the Slaughter, I escaped. I came here to be disarmed, to be unforged. Instead, I found the Library. I have been here ever since. Reading."

"Reading?"

"I will show you," he says. "But first we need to get moving. There are many Glystfell around this part of the city. Bigger and worse than the one I have just burned. Now, I'm going to lift your friend. Please refrain from putting an arrow in me."

"Very well," I say, sliding the arrow back into my quiver and shouldering the bow.

He scoops Ethra up with ease, as if it is just Skin-Ethra he is lifting, and starts walking back the way we have come.

"The Library is this way, in the West Streets. It is a little safer there."

I catch up with him, but struggle to keep pace. He has a long stride.

When I am beside him, he glances my way, then stops walking, his mouth hanging slack.

"Oh," I say. "That. The statue."

His voice drops to a whisper, and he says, "The Dracafysian."

"What?"

I do not know the word, but somehow it seems familiar. It fills me with dread, lifting the hairs on my arms and the back of my neck.

"In the old tongue it means 'She Who Drives Out Monsters'," says Madec.

"Be careful with my friend," I say because he looks as if he is about to drop Ethra onto the broken road at his feet.

"We should get to the Library," he says, lifting Ethra higher and securing her against his chest. "Then we can talk."

The further east we go, the less rundown everything appears. The buildings cease to sag, the road uncrumbles. There are trees planted along the roadside, and some are in blossom.

"The Glyst lingers here," says Madec. "But it is not wild Glyst. It is what some Maradyns called 'mild' or 'gentle' Glyst." He nods to a tower ahead of us. "We are here."

The tower is made of the same white stone as the walls. It is four storeys high and capped with a copper dome turned green by the elements. It is twice the diameter of our roundhouse back in

Gafol. There are many windows cut into the blockwork, but all are boarded up.

Madec leads us through a small door which opens at his approach. A spiral staircase takes us up through candlelit gloom. We emerge through a hole in the floor in the middle of a large room that is two-storeys tall and lined with dark wooden shelves that reach to the domed ceiling. The shelves are filled with books.

I have seen books before, of course. Once a scholar making a study of the flowers of the North of Abegan stayed over in Gafol. He had two books. One was full of words and illustrations about the flowers of the South of Abegan and had been written by the scholar's father many years before. The other was only half-filled with our visitor's accounts of what he had encountered so far of the North's flora. Then, when I was five or six, a storyteller came to Gafol. He read from a book about the exploits of Derenderlic, the first man who the gods made accidentally while under the influence of Seros' strongest brew. Derenderlic spent all his days making mischief until the gods sobered-up many years later and created Shiblessi, the first woman, who made the man calm and useful, for the most part.

I have seen books before, of course. But not this many. Hand on heart, I did not think this many books existed in all the world. There must be hundreds of them.

"Most are empty," says Madec, carrying Ethra to a bed off to one side, with a wooden chest at its foot. Next to the bed there is a small table with a single chair. There is a plate on the table with food still on it, some kind of stew. On the floor near the table and chair is a clay firebowl with an iron pot hanging above it from a three-legged stand. A little steam rises from the pot, and I can see glowing embers in the firebowl. This small area of the room appears to be the only part not dedicated to books and reading. There are chairs and tables scattered about, but all—including most of the chairs—are covered in books.

"The books are empty?" I say.

"Yes, for now." Madec opens the chest and begins pulling out bottles and jars. "Ah. This." He holds out a bottle no bigger than his thumb and pulls the stopper from it.

I can smell it from where I am standing, across the room.

"For now?" I say, beginning to feel stupid, and wondering if all my questions are going to be incredulous echoes of Madec's statements from now on.

"When the Cwalee came, the Maradyns put a Glyst on the books, fearful that their knowledge should fall into the hands of the invaders or even those people of Abegan who might cause untold harm with such learnings. The words vanished. It was as if they were never there. Not so much as a scratch on the paper or parchment, nor an indentation." He takes the stinking bottle to Ethra and holds it beneath her nose. "This will set her brain to dancing."

Ethra sits upright, as if her body has always been a right-angle and is simply snapping back into its original shape. Her eyes are wide and terrified.

"A rat!" she yelps. "As big as a gedding horse!"

"You have quite the tongue in your mouth," says Madec, smiling. "You do not look like a soldier, but you speak like one."

"Who are you?" she asks.

"Madec Teeg."

"Are you going to take me to see the Hollow?"

"I would hope not," he says, replacing the stopper and returning the bottle to the chest. "But if it is what you wish I have helped others."

"It is what I wish. Where are we?"

"A library," I say. "Filled with empty books."

"Most are empty," says Madec.

"An empty book seems like a silly thing," says Ethra.

"It does, doesn't it?" says Madec. "Although, for me, it is more of a frustrating thing. But when the words *bloom* out of the paper, it is the most wonderful thing."

"Bloom?" I say. I realise I am echoing his words again and so needlessly add, "What do you mean by that?"

"The Glyst that hid the words is fading, bit by bit. When it does, the books reveal their secrets."

"How do you know?" asks Ethra, pivoting so her legs are hanging from the bed.

"That's the frustrating aspect of it all," says Madec. "It is a page here or there. Sometimes less. A paragraph or even a paltry sentence. And I don't know which books or pages have yielded up their treasures. I have to work my way through every book, one page at a time."

I look at the crammed shelves.

"That's an *impossible* task," I say.

"It is," says Madec. "And, yet, here I am. And here *you* are."

He walks toward me, staring, taking in every detail of my face.

"It *is* you. The Dracafysian. It cannot be a coincidence." And then he smiles. "I always thought there was a little of El in that statue's visage. I'd just assumed there was a common fierceness, that was all, and that I was being wishful."

"Who is the Dracafysian?" says Ethra, standing, then sniffing at the contents of the cooking pot.

"Help yourself," says Madec. "It's still warm." He points to a chair and then says to me, "Sit."

I clear it of books, placing them on the adjacent table—itself already piled with books—and sit.

"The Dracafysian is your friend here," Madec says, turning briefly to Ethra, who is already ladling stew into a wooden bowl. "At least, it would very much seem that she is."

"But who is the Dracafysian?" I ask, failing to keep the impatience from my voice.

"Nobody really knows," says Madec.

It is all I can do not to roll my eyes and sigh with exasperation.

"There are many conflicting oral accounts and almost nothing written down," he continues. He glances at the shelves. "At least, little is written as yet." He pulls a chair up next to mine and sits. "There is one song, a round."

"*She stands at the Gates of Utlath, her finewolf at her side*," I say. "*She dies at the Gates of Utlath, her finewolf at her side. And forever more and ever after, every Glyster cried*."

A round. I remember it now, being sung as such. Just the same three lines, over and over.

"There are more lines," says Madec. "Heard rarely. *The Dracafysian comes in the night or day.*

All of us to save or slay. Smiling, roaring, she becomes our Queen. Or becomes the consort of the Gravene. I don't doubt there are more lines than this, but they are lost. Or, at the very least, undiscovered, invisible."

"The Gravene," I say. "Tell me about the Gravene."

Chapter 29

Dead Heavens

"You have heard the First Story," says Madec, sprinkling some dried herbs onto his stew.

"Of course," I say.

"I told it only a day or two ago," says Ethra.

"Then you know how the story sometimes changes a little here and there, as tellers embroider it for entertainment or steer it toward their own views, beliefs and feelings."

"It is rarely exactly the same twice," I say. "But always broadly similar. And, at heart, in its foundations, identical."

"Quite," says Madec. "There is a version on these shelves, that is very different, that diverges significantly. That version tells of the Glyst. That version tells of the Gravene."

Again, the name itself chills me. The Gravene.

"Tell it," I say.

And so he does.

In the beginning, there was nothing

There was no thing and there was no time.

And then arose the Moment.

And being the only thing that was, the Moment was Everything.

And it was Everything all at once.

It was as a roaring, crashing wave, obliterating the nothing in an instant.

But in its violent suddenness, it created, instead of nothing, the shuddering chaos known as the Dwolma.

The Moment sat at the centre of the Dwolma and the Moment was the Dwolma.

And the Moment was afraid and could find no peace.

And so the Moment began to bring order to the chaos, which was the Dwolma, which was the Moment.

It began by creating Heaven.

Heaven was a calmness in the midst of chaos.

But the Moment found the calmness of Heaven only served to accentuate the shuddering chaos beyond its edges.

And so the Moment created another heaven.

But this was not enough; still it only served to accentuate the seething chaos of the Dwolma.

And so the Moment created another heaven.

Even so, it was not enough.

And so the Moment created a multitude of heavens.

And even though there were now so many heavens the Dwolma was as a ribbon threading through the slim places between them, it was still not enough.

*And so the Moment created within each heaven
a wealth of distractions: mountains, meadows and
seas; deserts, forests and swamps; valleys, tundras
and plateaus.*

And it was not enough. Still, it was not enough.

*And so the Moment created the gods of each
heaven. And to the Moment's delight, the gods,
because they were of the Moment, began their own
makings.*

Skies, stars, worlds.

*And they made of each world a heaven, with its
own mountains, meadows and seas; deserts, forests
and swamps; valleys, tundras and plateaus.*

*And as the Moment had made the gods of each
heaven, the gods of each heaven made the peoples
of each world.*

*And as the gods were of the Moment, so the
peoples of each world were of the Moment, though
the Moment was made weak in them, as blood is
made weak in water.*

*The Weak Moment that is in all the peoples is
known as the Glyst.*

Madec mops his bowl with a piece of bread.

"There are pages waiting to be filled after that,"
he says. "And then a single page, itself
incomplete."

*The Dwolma, stretched thin between the
Heavens of the Moment's making and the skies,*

stars and worlds of the gods' making, grew
resentful. Once, there had only been the Moment
and the Dwolma, and they had been of one
another. Now the Dwolma seemed hardly anything
at all. And resentment turned to anger. Anger to
fury. And the Dwolma remembered when the
Moment had been afraid of the seething,
shuddering chaos. And the Dwolma wished that it
were so again.

The Dwolma, having observed the Moment's
makings, had learnt something of the art itself, and
so set to forging its own creations.

The Dwolma made its own heaven, which it
called Efeld-Drah, which means Web of Dust. And
Efeld-Drah was as a thread that wound through
the spaces between all the heavens of the Moment's
making. And the Dwolma populated Efeld-Drah
with its own gods. And the Dwolma's gods made
their own world, which they called G'medella,
which means Madness. And G'medella was not as
a sphere, but as a thread that wound through the
spaces between all the worlds of the Moment's
gods' making. And the Dwolma's gods populated
G'medella with its own peoples.

And amongst the peoples of the world created
by the gods of Efeld-Drah are the Cwalee.

And chief amongst the gods of Efeld-Drah is the
Gravene.

"And that is all the book has yielded so far," says Madec. "It doesn't even have a title or an author yet. Just the words I have told to you."

I realise I haven't touched my stew and eat a spoonful out of politeness more than appetite.

"We should go," says Ethra. "It will be dark soon and I would have this done."

My head is so full of heavens and gods and worlds that it takes me a second to assemble her words into a meaning.

"You are sure?" says Madec. "That you wish to be rid of the Glyst?"

"Not rid," says Ethra. "Free. Free of it."

"Then you are right. We should go now."

"Aren't you going to try to persuade her otherwise, Madec?" I ask.

"No," he says. "It is her Glyst. Her life. Her choice. It is not for me or anyone to gainsay that. No matter how much will be lost as a consequence. I have been a slave of bad people and a slave of good people. In both cases, I was still a slave. And to be a slave is to be without choice."

I think of Cass, the scars on his body. I think of how I fear the Jarl, how even my father, strong and skilled, fears the Jarl.

I sigh.

"If you are sure, Ethra," I say.

"I am," she replies.

But, for an instant, I think I see a flicker of doubt.

"You are?"

"I am."

Perhaps I imagined it.

"I will tell you more on the way to the docks," says Madec. "I will tell you of the Book of Tungol Witt."

As we leave his tower, Madec draws his sword and tells me to have my bow ready.

"It is not safe now," he says.

"It wasn't safe before," I say, remembering the rat thing.

"It is less so now."

"Good to know." And then I wonder why Madec has his sword drawn when he could set fire to any attackers with ease. "Why the sword?"

"My Glyst is exhausted for the next few hours. Such a feat as the one you witnessed is draining."

"So, you were bluffing earlier?"

"I was."

"I could have put an arrow in you and there would have been little you could have done about it?"

"Nothing I could have done about it, in point of fact. The Glyst is unreliable and inconsistent. A certain amount of bluster is sometimes necessary."

I recall Cass's blather about Luthyl, the Spirit of Love, and Glystspores. Bluster can indeed be useful.

"Who is Tungol Witt?" I ask.

"Not 'is', 'was'," says Madec. "He was a prophet. A seer."

"He saw the future?"

"He fancied he did, And I fancy he was right."

"And what did he see?"

"Among other things, he saw now," says Madec. "He wrote many years ago. Decades, perhaps centuries ago. His far future was our present. He wrote of how the Cwalee would come to our world. And he was right. He wrote of how the Cwalee would come and drain the Glyst from all the Maradyns of Utlath, of how they would drain the Glyst from *all* the Maradyns of the great cities of the world."

Somewhere, something howls. The howl echoes. Or it is answered by another howl. It is impossible to tell which.

"But the Cwalee invasion was only the beginning, according to Witt's visions. They did not come because they hungered for the Glyst. They came with the purpose of taking the Glyst from the world."

"Why?" asks Ethra.

We arrive at the place where the rat thing attacked. There is little left of it now. What hasn't turned to ash is being devoured by rats of normal proportions, except for their tails, which are absurdly long—ten times the length of their bodies.

"To render the world defenceless," Madec continues. "So that the Gravene might take it with ease. As it has taken other worlds."

"Other worlds?"

"Yes. Many. And other heavens. Before it takes a world, the Gravene takes its heaven. Its heaven and its gods. That is its strategy. According to Witt, anyway. The gods are powerful, but they are few. And while the peoples of a world might call upon the gods for support, the gods do not call upon the peoples. First, the Gravene sends the Cwalee to the world, to drain it of its Glyst. The Gravene goes away for a time and forges from the leeched Glyst a weapon. The Bord-e-Lak. Next it turns the Bord-e-Lak on the gods, destroying them and laying waste to their heaven. And then, finally, when all of that is done, it takes the world. Witt wrote that he saw this happen time and again, in waking, fevered dreams. He saw this happen to other worlds and then, in his final vision, to ours."

"But why didn't the gods stop the Cwalee from taking the Glyst?" says Ethra. "Then the Gravene would not be able to create this Bord-e-Lak and turn it against the gods."

"Witt asked this, too," says Madec. "He wrote that he asked the question of the ghost of a long-dead god. The dead god, 'in a voice that was as light and music mixed', told him that the gods have always been troubled by the Glyst, threatened by it, resentful of it, and when the Cwalee came to take it away from the peoples, they were secretly pleased and did nothing, and so were responsible through inaction for their own downfall. Witt calls this the Great Mistake, and he saw it repeated time and again. Dead worlds, dead gods, dead heavens."

Dead heavens.

I remember what I saw through Eftas Hilder's eyes. That grey place with its faceless men with bodies seemingly made from sticky, steaming rope. I recall what Cass said, and Ethra and even Hilder himself.

Cass: *There were no Unrim. And there was no River of Honey.*

Ethra: *Tiny grey mushrooms sprouted from everything. I could feel them on my tongue. I could feel them under my eyelids when I blinked. It was silent.*

Hilder: *I can still taste it. It tasted as it looked, grey and damp.*

They were describing a dead heaven.

"How long after a heaven falls does its world follow?" I ask.

"A ten-year or less, according to Witt."

I stop walking. A few seconds later, Madec, noticing I am no longer beside him, also stops. He looks back at me."

"What?" he says.

"Our heaven has fallen," I say. "Our gods are vanquished."

His face turns pale, and fear darkens his eyes.

"How do you know this?" he says.

"I have seen it," I say.

"Seen it?" asks Madec.

"Yes."

"And I," says Ethra. "The Fields of Wealm were grey as ash."

Madec runs a hand through his hair, looks to the darkening sky and then down at his feet.

"Then we must hurry," he says. "We must get your friend to the Hollow that we might get back to the Library and discuss what we need to do next."

"And what do we need to do next?" I ask.

"Raise an army," says Madec. "An army of Glysters."

Chapter 30

The Hollow

The rot we've witnessed so far in the buildings
of Utlath is nothing compared to what we see as we
near the docks.

There is hardly a building that isn't collapsing
into itself, slimy, oozing, stinking. A faintly
luminous algae covers everything, and straggling
weeds sprout from every crack. Here and there,
among the ruins, pale, bloated, amphibious
creatures squat, licking fat flies from the air with
their sudden tongues. The air itself feels damp. It
coats me like a cold sweat.

The road begins to slope downward and widens,
the rotten buildings fall to nothing but sodden
debris, and the docks lifts into view. It is crammed
with ships, a hundred or more. Or what is left of
them. A blighted forest of masts. There are galleys
on their sides, oars reaching up like the arms of
drowning men. The jetties that lead out to the ships
look treacherous, missing more planks than they
possess and reminding me of the abandoned bridge
over the Woever on the edge of Gafol. It looks as if
the place was evacuated in haste—as doubtless it
was—with crates, barrels and carts scattered about

in disarray and rotting into puddles of their own decay.

Everything shimmers with rot. The ships so much so they no longer look as if they have been fashioned from strong timber. Rather, they look as if they are made from the flesh of some vast sea-dwelling creature. Improperly cured, the flesh has decayed until it appears almost a thick liquid held upright by Glystwork. They look as if a single prick with a sword's tip might cause them to burst and cascade down into the sea.

"Where are they to be found?" says Ethra. "The Hollow."

There is an undeniable tremor of fear in her voice.

"They will come soon enough," says Madec. "I suspect they have already caught the scent of our Glyst and will be rising from their quarters."

"Quarters? They are aboard the ships?" I ask.

"Yes. They cannot bear to be in Utlath. They do not want to be reminded that they were once the extraordinary, illustrious and celebrated Maradyns and now they are... well, you'll see."

Ethra looks out across the docks at the rotting ships.

"I don't see anything," she says.

"Patience," I say. "You have come this far, waited this long."

"I would wait no longer," says Ethra and puffs herself up. "I want this curse gone."

"There," says Madec, pointing to a ship some two hundred yards out. It is a slumped and sorry thing.

"I still don't see anything," says Ethra.

Nor do I.

"The foremast," says Madec. "See how it seems to move?"

He's right. It seems to undulate and twist. And then I realise there are... *things* crawling up and round it. From this distance, they are just clots of shadow. They rise up the mast, thirty or more of them, and when they reach the uppermost yard— still miraculously intact—they *leap*. They land on the mizzenmast of a vessel closer to us and slither down to the deck. They scuttle across the deck, skipping over holes in the timbers, and up the bowsprit, from the sagging end of which they leap onto the poop deck of another ship. In this fashion, they make their way to shore, gathering on the jetty directly ahead of us.

They jibber among themselves for a minute, then one of them detaches from the others and scampers toward us. As it approaches, it ceases to be a clot of shadow. I wish it had remained so.

Clad in a filthy robe, it is the size of a toddling child, but wrinkled as the oldest of men. In fact, it is more wrinkled than any old man I have ever seen. It is as if someone has somehow made a person from a potato then left it in the dark for many months. There are no eyes to speak of, just bruised indents as if made by pushing a thumb into the thing's too-yielding flesh. The nose is a hole. The mouth, a slash. Most horrible of all are the pale roots that sprout from the furrows of its shrivelled face and from the backs of its hands and the tops of its shoeless feet. The roots *move*, as water weeds move in a river's current. They strain toward Ethra, Madec and me, and I know that it is not us that attracts them but our Glyst.

It stops a few yards from us. The slash of a mouth widens, and a tongue that is more like a grey slug licks non-existent lips. Even though it has no eyes, I can feel it staring at us, staring *into* us.

I find myself drawing my bowstring to the anchor point and training my arrow on the creature's chest. From the corner of my eye, I see Ethra's hand go to the grip of her sword.

I do not know what I expect it to sound like when it speaks. Ancient? Mouldering? But it is neither of those things. Its voice is soft and clear. Not the voice of an 'it' at all, but the voice of a young woman.

"I am sorry we are such an awful sight," she says. "Please do not be frightened."

"I am not frightened," says Ethra, but her tone suggests otherwise.

"We will not harm you. They call us the Hollow and Glystleeches and worse, but we are none of those things. We are the Maradyn, as we always were. But powerless now. During the Abundance we showered the land with gifts, with healings and help. Now, the only gift we can give is peace if the Glyst is a source of suffering for its possessor. The stories have us feeding out of hunger, but that is not so. We feed to serve, as the Maradyn have always served the people of the world."

"She speaks true," says Madec. "There is no need of weapons."

I lower my bow and replace my arrow in its quiver. Ethra's hand moves from her sword.

"And how are you, Madec?" says the old Maradyn.

"Well, thank you. And yourself?"

"Terrible, as always," she says cheerfully, the slash of a mouth lifting in a smile. "But I am alive and that is quite a thing."

"It is," says Madec, smiling himself. "Quite a thing and always a surprise."

The Maradyn turns to Ethra and me.

"Which of you wishes for peace?" she asks.

"Me," says Ethra.

The Maradyn steps forward, her root-sprouting hand extended.

Trying—and failing—to conceal her reluctance, Ethra shakes her hand. The pale roots extend and probe at Ethra's fingers.

"That tickles," she says.

"I'm sorry," she says. "They are impertinent things, these tendrils. They do not do as I bid." She withdraws her hand and conceals it, along with her other, in her tattered, stained robe. "My name is Hrof," she says. "Hrof Arstafas. My Glyst was Touch Learning. I could put my finger to the temple of an old shipwright, and I would know all the intricacies of shipbuilding. I could touch the forehead of an apothecary and know the precise ingredients and measurements of any decoction, elixir or tincture that was within their knowledge." She chuckles. "Once, when I was a child, I touched a squirrel and knew where he had stored all his heartnuts for the winter!" Her delight fades quickly. "All gone now, of course, along with most of my memory. Now, all I can do, all any of us Maradyns of old can do," she casts a glance over her shoulder at the gathered shadows on the jetty, "is take that which is not wanted, that which is causing pain." She looks up at Ethra, and somehow, a kindliness appears on her strange face. "Are you in pain, child?"

"I am," says Ethra.

"Then let us get to this," says Hrof. She turns to Madec. "I will see you again in the morning."

"In the morning?" I say, as Madec nods.

"It is a slow process if it is to be painless," says Hrof. "The Glyst is everywhere in the Glyster. It connects the soul with the heart with the mind with the muscles with the bones with the blood. It is not easily separated."

"Then I will stay," I say. "I will wait."

"That isn't wise," says Hrof. "It will be full dark soon, and this is a most dangerous place for those who do not know it. Even Madec does not stay out long after dark."

I look up at the sky and realise it is already getting dark. I can see two stars. One is reddish, the other yellow. The Mismatched Eyes from the constellation of Memynd, God of Madness. They are always the first stars to show themselves as night begins to fall. The others will make themselves known within the hour.

"She's right," says Madec. "We will go back to the Library. I have a great deal to tell you."

"It's okay," says Ethra. "I'll be fine. I'm not scared."

"You sound scared," I say.

"Well, maybe I am a little. Or more than a little. But this is what I want, and I would have it done before I change my mind."

"Do you wish to change your mind?"

"No," says Ethra. "But I might, the more we dally. And I would regret that, I think."

"She will be safe with us," says Hrof. "I give you my word, as Hrof Arstafas, the Glystmistress as was, once know not just throughout Abegan but in many countries of the world." She smiles up at me. It is as sweet a smile as I have seen since my mother passed. "My solemn, sacred word," she says.

"Very well," I say, and go to Ethra. I put my arms around her and pull her close. She hugs me hard.

"Thank you, Alys Clainh," she says. "For saving my life, for returning my life and for bringing me here though it put you in much danger. In my home of Mella, such acts would make us sisters. There would be a ceremony, and you would after be called Alys Clainh-Kell kin of Ethra, and I would be called Ethra Kell-Clainh kin of Alys." She hugs me harder. "Thank you."

"You are welcome, Ethra Kell-Clainh," I say. "My kin. My sister."

We hold one another for a long time and would have carried on doing so, but Madec says, "We should go, Alys. Utlath becomes more dangerous by the minute after dark."

Ethra pulls away, plants a kiss on my cheek and turns to Hrof.

"Let's be done with this," she says.

"Very well," says Hrof. She turns to the other Maradyns and waves them over.

As one they come, the details of their pale, folded faces coming into focus as they advance. They do not seem so grotesque now that I have heard Hrof speak and seen her smile. In fact, they do not seem grotesque at all. Rather, they seem like strange vessels of concentrated kindness, agents of gentleness. And they seem sad, too, the form heartbreak might take if it somehow manifested as a physical being.

They gather in a circle around Ethra and begin talking in soft, sweet voices. I do not recognise the language they speak.

Madec puts a hand on my shoulder.

"Let's go," he says.

I smile at Ethra. She smiles back. It is a brave smile.

I turn away and begin walking back up the road, away from the docks, away from Ethra and the sweet, almost singing, voices of the ancient Maradyn.

As we pass the dead rat-thing—mostly bones now—I ask Madec, "If Heaven is fallen, where are the dead?"

"I don't know," he says.

"The Fields of Wealm were to be their reward, their rest…"

"Best not think on it. The books may yield the answer in time."

"My mother…" I say.

"As I say, best not think on it."

But I can think of nothing else. Has the Gravene taken them?

And then another possibility enters my head. I wish it hadn't. What if those faceless things… what if *they* were the dead?

I push *all* thoughts from my mind then, and focus on putting one foot ahead of the other.

We are halfway back to the Library, the wound in my thigh aching once more as the balm Cass purchased in Leax begins to wane, when a figure darts from the shadows between two buildings.

It happens so quickly.

A sword blade flashes.

Madec drops to his knees, his own sword falling to the ground.

And Slek Mydra strides toward me, grinning.

Chapter 31

The Same River

Mydra says something in that deathly quiet voice of his, but I don't hear it over the sound of my heartbeat, over the roar of blood in my ears.

I loose an arrow, and it strikes his shoulder.

He winces, but only a little. The blood-red leather of his Sceada armour is thick, and I have wasted my chance. There is barely enough time to select another arrow, and none to nock, draw and loose it. I cast my bow aside, jump back and draw my sword.

Madec looks at me. The lower half of his face is red with blood. There's a deep, wide wound to his chest. I can see bone among the gore, gleaming white. It reminds me of my father's deathwound, inflicted by the slite's antlers, and why does that seem like years ago now?

Madec raises his hands. They are gloved in flame.

"Burn him!" I say, pointing my sword tip at Mydra. "Burn him!"

But Madec doesn't burn him. Madec's eyes roll back until only the whites are visible, and he falls face first to the floor. And then Madec starts to burn.

"One less Glystgedder in the world," says Mydra, giving his sword a flourish. "One less specimen of Glystfilth staining all our lives. Good. And soon we'll be less another."

He says more, but I hear none of it. My heart, erupting with fear now, has made my pulse all but deafening.

He heaves his sword at me and, more from instinct than intent, I parry. A mistake. He is stronger than me, his blade heavier. The jolt from the blow almost disarms me but I manage, just, to retain my sword.

I try to recall El's training:

When an opponent is stronger than you, keep moving. Tire him out. Wait for an opening.

And then I remember another piece of advice, delivered on the same cold, damp morning:

If an opponent is better than you, run. It is as simple as that.

Slek Mydra is both stronger *and* better. He has fought in battles, in wars. I dread to think how many people he has slain. And not just people: beasts and monsters.

But I cannot run. The wound in my leg means Mydra will catch me with ease. I would not win the Five Feathers today. I would not win any race.

Then another pearl of wisdom from that seemingly years-ago training session:

And if you cannot outrun him, and you must
fight, then be sure to have allies. That is why you
endured the Ritual of the Seven Cuts and the Seven
Cups, that your father, my brother, would have an
ally when he hunted in the Freewood. The making
of allies is one of the greatest skills a warrior can
possess, equal to their ability with sword, shield,
spear and bow.

I look around.

I have no allies.

I am alone. And I am scared. When will I ever
not be scared?

Mydra lunges at me with his blade. I sidestep,
then slash at him. But he is quick as well as strong,
and my weapon finds nothing but air. He lunges
again and I skip back several paces. The wound in
my thigh chooses this precise moment to awaken
fully, and I almost fall.

"You can't win, girl," says Mydra, and his
voice is calm, reasonable. "Drop your sword, and I
will take you back to Gafol, to the Jarl. He might
show you mercy."

We circle one another.

"And what of my father?" I say, my voice
tremulous with fear. "The Jarl will show him no
mercy."

"Your father?" says Mydra, and there is a note
of pity in his voice, and for the life of me I cannot

decide if it is true or mocking. "Your father will be dead a day or two from now. I sent the last of my men back to deliver a message to my Jarl. The Clainh girl is a Glyster, my man will say, and her father is a liar."

"You're the liar!" I say. But then I remember Cass saying he had heard there were four men looking for me when he went in search of spedig in Awlen. Mydra, Hilder, Syrunn… and another. Another, conspicuous by his absence.

"The Sceada do not lie," he says. "We do not lie. And we do not betray. If I say something is so, then it is so. Your father is, to all intents and purposes, already dead. You underestimated me, girl, and that will be your undoing. How do you think I found you here? Luck? No. I knew your friend, the Scur, was seeking money. I knew you were headed east. It is not possible to make much of a fortune from fish, so it could only be Utlath that he sought and its bounty of grefa stones. If you had not underestimated me, I would still have had need of a tracker. And your father would yet live."

And now I am so much filled with fear—for myself, for my father—that I can barely hold my sword. Fear is in my muscles, weakening them. It is in my heart, trying to claw its way out. It is in my lungs, displacing every ounce of air. It is in my mind, making me think of the Ritual, making me think that I am *still* enduring the ritual, still strung up like a pig or foorstig, the seventh cut (which is really two cuts) having just been delivered across my thighs and blood running into my mouth, up my nose, into my eyes.

Mydra lurches toward me, swinging his sword once, twice. Both times I dodge, the second time by such a small measure the tip of his blade tears the arm of my tunic.

I am dizzy with fear.

Why didn't I ask El, when I had the chance, what the cure for fear was, how it might be overcome? Was it embarrassment that kept the question in my head, that prevented it from finding its way to my tongue?

Am I to die of embarrassment?

Would El even have had a lesson for me?

But then I remember I *have* received a lesson in the nature of fear.

Not from El, but from the man who is pressing me back with every slash and thrust of his sword.

Slek Mydra.

The words he said to dying Hilder. The words he said to me.

Afraid? So what? So what if you are afraid? It matters not. You think I am never afraid? That I do not experience fear? Fear and courage are the same river. When you are afraid, you are swimming against the current. When you are brave, you are swimming with the current, letting it take you were it will. Either way, you are in the river. And the river can bring pain, suffering, death. But it is easier to swim with the current. Once you realise this and embrace the fear, accept that it is simply... there, you have the makings of a warrior. It is not the fear that paralyses. It is the battling of it. So say we Sceada, anyway.

Fear and courage. The same river.

And the Sceada do not lie. If they say something is so, then it is so.

The same river.

I am submerged in it. And so is Slek Mydra, who even now is smiling. Smiling and seemingly fearless. But he is not fearless. He is swimming in fear. The only difference is he is doing so willingly, not battling against it.

And then the fear is no longer weakening my muscles, no longer clawing at my heart, no longer emptying my lungs or taking my mind back to the Ritual of the Seven Cuts and the Seven Cups. The fear is just *there*. As the sky is there. As the air I breathe is there.

"It is not the fear that paralyses," I say. "It is the battling of it."

This causes Mydra to raise an eyebrow. To hesitate.

I lunge forward, jabbing my sword at his midsection.

The move catches him by surprise and he fails to parry.

My sword tip punctures his armour. But only by half an inch.

As I draw back, I swipe at his weapon arm and feel a satisfying resistance.

He grunts, shuffling back out of the reach of my sword.

"First blood is yours, daughter and son of Aryc Clainh. I salute you." He tosses the blade to his other hand. "But the Sceada fight with both hands. And that is the last blood you shall draw."

He charges at me, roaring.

I smile.

Less than a minute ago, I would have run. I wouldn't have been able to help myself. Fear would have driven me to it.

And I am still afraid. The fear is all around me.

But it does not matter. It is simply… *there*.

I fight. I fight, though I know I cannot win. I fight with clarity.

When he thrusts, I dodge. When he slashes, I duck or step back. Occasionally, I parry, but only when I can use the Sceada's own momentum to divert his blade. I counterattack when I can, finding openings here and there, jabbing into them and slashing as I retreat.

Twice I catch him, once on his right forearm, once to the left wrist. Each time, the cut is deep enough to extract a grunt and send Mydra into a brief retreat.

But he is still smiling and shows no sign of tiring.

I, on the other hand, am beginning to weary.

"You are flagging, Alys. Perhaps drop the sword now. The Jarl may let you live."

"You are wrong about that," I say. "Just as you were wrong about my first cut being the last."

A cloud of anger shadows Mydra's face.

"I will give you one last chance to lay down your sword, Clainh," he says through gritted teeth.

"Do you believe the Jarl will let me live?" I ask.

The Sceada cannot lie. It is not in their nature. And so Mydra says nothing.

I repeat the question.

Myra shrugs.

"No," he says. "I do not believe that he will."

I smile.

"To the death, then?" he says.

"To the death," I say.

I attack him with such savagery, such ferocity, that I do not recognise myself.

Steel clashes against steel so hard, sparks illuminate the gloom.

"That's the spirit!" roars Mydra, a grin almost splitting his face.

I wonder if my face now has the same countenance as that of my likeness at the Dead City's gates: rage, determination, madness.

I strike at him again and again, and he parries each blow, but step by step I am driving him back. Every bone in my hand and arm thrums with pain. I can feel blood running down my leg from my reopened arrow wound.

And I don't care.

I couldn't stop if I wanted to.

For one foolish moment, I believe I can win, that I can kill Slek Mydra, this fierce Sceada warrior who has been in more battles than I have years in my bones.

And then my sword—my father's sword— breaks.

Chapter 32

A Final Cruelty

I stare at the broken blade and, for one ridiculous second, I worry that my father will be disappointed with me for not having looked after it properly.

And then the Sceada slashes at the arm holding the half-sword. It is not as deep as it could have been—I don't doubt Mydra could have lopped off my arm at the elbow—but it is deep enough that I drop my weapon.

He lunges at me, grips me by the throat and lifts me from the ground.

He does all of this with such ease that I know I could never have beaten him, no matter how many nicks and slices I delivered, no matter how much blood I drew. I am not strong enough yet. I am not good enough yet.

But at least I am not filled with fear as I was.

I punch his arm, finding the places my sword opened up. I punch over and over, until my knuckles are red not only with his blood, but with mine. I kick at his chest and belly, connecting again and again. But his armour does more damage to my feet than I can ever hope to do to him. I might leave him with a bruise or two, but that is all.

But I don't stop kicking or punching until the energy goes out of me, as a candle flame goes out when it has burned the last of its tallow.

And even as I hang there, struggling to draw breath past the tightening grip of his hand, I am not filled with fear. I am swimming in it. I am swimming *with* it.

"You fought well," says Mydra. "You would best most of the men of Gafol. I would put heavy coin on you, Alys. It is a shame. I would like to see what you would grow into. But I am here on my Jarl's business."

He points the tip of his sword at my chest, my heart. It is to be a quick death, then. A merciful death. He pulls back his arm… then stops.

Confusion creases his brow.

He drops the sword. It is heavy and makes a sound like chiming bells as it strikes the stones of the road.

Next, he drops me. I land on my feet, but my wounded leg betrays me, and I continue down to the ground.

He turns, facing away from me.

There is a knife sticking out of his back, between the shoulder blades. It is sunk in up to its hilt. The handle is pretty, white bone, carved in the shape of one of the Sea Ladies that are said to swim off the coast at Leax, with tail and scales where legs should be.

The knife belongs to Casmel Durn, to *Cass*.

I cannot see him past Mydra, but I hear him speak.

"Good evening, Slek Mydra," he says with good cheer. "I'm the boy who made a fool of you in Awlen."

Mydra roars. His hands scrabble for the knife in his back, almost finding it.

Legs useless, I drag myself to my father's broken sword, seize the grip as tight as my waning strength will allow, and slash its incomplete blade across the back of the Sceada's thighs. One cut that is really two.

He turns back to me now, still roaring, still smiling.

He reaches down and picks up his sword.

As he bends, I see Cass, his own sword drawn, striding forward, preparing to finish him.

But we have surprised the Sceada twice, and he will not allow himself to be outwitted a third time. He rises quickly, bringing his elbow back in a swift and brutal motion. I hear it crunch into Cass's face. He cries out in pain, and I see him crumple to the floor, his nose a bloody mess, his eyes rolling wildly for a second before unconsciousness takes him.

I turn away from the scene and begin pulling myself toward my bow, beyond which is all that remains of Madec: a pile of smouldering ash in the shape of a man.

I don't get very far.

Mydra's foot comes down hard on my wounded leg and pins me to the ground. I stretch a hand toward my bow, but my fingertips strain an inch from it.

I can hear the pain in his voice when he says, "I am less sorry than I was to put an end to your life, Alys Clainh. But I am still sorry."

He lifts his foot from my thigh.

"Turn," he says. "I would not put a sword in your back, even if you and your comrade would mine."

I twist myself onto my back.

Mydra stands over me, sword in hand. He is not smiling now. He looks grim and regretful.

"Be done with it," I say.

There is no fear in my voice, and my heart is not beating as hard as perhaps it should.

Then I see Ethra's face appear above Mydra's head. She looks angry.

She is floating in the air.

I consider the possibility I am hallucinating, that pain, exhaustion and the prospect of death have made me delirious.

Then Ethra grabs Mydra's shoulders and drags him upward.

Shock wipes the regret from his face, and he drops his sword.

They hang ten yards above me, the Sceada's legs kicking.

He reaches behind him. At first, I think he is trying to get to Ethra. But then I realise it's the knife he's after. Cass's knife, buried between his shoulder blades.

I scuttle back, sitting up as I do so, until I am beside my bow. I pick it up, nock an arrow.

The knife is in Mydra's hand now, the blade dripping with his own blood.

I draw back the bowstring and surprise myself when I succeed, despite my exhaustion, in pulling it to the anchor point.

Mydra's arm arcs back toward Ethra.

I aim; then I loose the arrow.

It strikes Mydra's arm and, with a noise more howl than roar, he drops the knife.

Ethra takes him higher.

Twenty yards. Thirty. Forty. Fifty.

And then she drops him.

He makes no noise as he falls. He just stretches out his arms, accepting his fate.

I watch his swift descent, not even looking away when his body strikes the broken stones of the road between Cass and me, refusing to cover my ears to the sound of his cracking bones, the wet slap of blood.

Using my bow as a staff, I stand and make my way over to the dead Sceada.

Only he isn't dead.

His bloody mouth opens and closes. His eyes dart this way and that, as if tracking the erratic trail of a housefly, and then they lock onto mine.

His voice little more than a fragmented wheeze, he says, "It… is… well."

His eyes clip shut. His jaw drops wide, releasing its tide of blood.

At the same moment as Mydra leaves our world, Cass returns.

He sits up, his hand to his face.

"By nobe," he says. "By nobe ib bokem."

"It might be an improvement," says Ethra, landing lightly beside him. Then, suddenly serious, "Is that… Madec?" She points at the man-shaped pile of glowing, smoking ashes.

"Yes," I say.

"Could you…?" she says.

Could I? I don't know. There is so little of him.

"I don't think so. I don't know."

"But you should try," says Ethra. "If you have the strength."

I don't have the strength. I barely have any strength.

But I try.

I kneel next to the pile of ashes. I feel a warmth from it, as you would from a hearth fire that is dwindling near evening's end.

But how am I to find and release my Glyst when I am too tired for rage? Last time, when I raised Hilder, I found my anger by locating my fear that was coiled about it like a fensnake. But now it seems I have no fear within me. Master Fensnake has slithered into the waters and away. There are no signs pointing to my Glyst, no keys to its door, nor even any moss growing up high on the trees giving an indication of the direction in which it might be found.

Where is my Glyst?

The Glyst is everywhere in the Glyster. It connects the soul with the heart with the mind with the muscles with the bones with the blood.

The words of Hrof Arstafas.

My blood.

My bones.

My muscles.

My mind.

My heart.

My soul.

There.

There it is.

Where it always was: *everywhere*.

Everywhere in me.

My Glyst.

I direct it, shepherd it, from my blood, bones, muscles, mind, heart and soul, down into my fingertips, and I push my hands into the burning ash that is all that is left of Madec Teeg.

And then I am in the Nowhere once more, that place where there are no troubles because there are no things. And again, I want to stay. But maybe not quite so much as before, maybe only a little this time, as one might wish to have a nap, a brief respite from labour.

And again the ripple comes. But it seems bigger this time, more violent, as if I am further from the shore and closer to the point of collision. Even though I have no body in this Nowhere, I *feel* it.

The stone has hit the lake.

It is about the Big Things. The Gods.

Suddenly, I am back in the Dead City, back in Utlath as was.

I turn to the shattered mess that was Slek Mydra. I point my right hand at him.

"It is coming," says the Sceada's slack, hanging mouth, despite the blood that fills it. "It is coming. The Gravene."

The pale-pink lifelight lifts from Mydra's impact-distorted head. His already sagging body collapses until it is just a skin filled with almost nothing.

The light floats toward me. I smell blackberries and rose petals. I reach to touch it.

"It's too late," says Ethra.

I look first at her, then at the remains of Madec. But there are no remains.

A wind that seems to have come into existence for the express purpose is carrying them in a spiralling blue-grey cloud down the broken road toward the docks.

"No!" I say. "There was still so much he needed to tell me. So much that I need to know."

I touch Mydra's lifelight and, with a sweep of my arm, send it after Madec's ashen remains.

But the lifelight resists. It veers right where I would have it go forward; then it disappears between the very buildings from which the Sceada had ambushed us. For a moment, its pink glow lingers in the shadows, and then it is gone.

I can't help feeling this is Slek Mydra's final revenge. And I can't help but, on some level of myself I never knew existed, admire his final cruelty.

A long time passes.

It gets darker, colder.

"What now?" says Ethra.

"Now?" I say. "Now, we build an army. We build an army to fight the Gravene. An army of Glysters."

Chapter 33

The Beginning

We return to Madec's Library.

I dress the wound Mydra inflicted upon my arm. Then, as I reset Cass's nose as best I can, I share with him all that Madec Teeg had told.

"I am absent for just a few hours," he says. "And you've gone from Alys Clainh to this… Dracafysian. You've been busy."

He is trying to make light of it, but there is a look in his rapidly bruising eyes of bewilderment.

"It is a lot to take in," I say. "Perhaps it's best to put some sleep on top of it. Besides, who knows how much of it is true and how much is the fancy of storytellers?"

He nods, the bewilderment still in his eyes.

I turn to Ethra and say, "You changed your mind. You kept your Glyst."

"Yes."

"Why?"

I don't know what I expect her to say.

"I like flying," she says. "And my skin hasn't come loose for days now. But mostly it's the flying. The Maradyn had just begun the ceremony. I was lying on my back and I was looking up at the sky and I thought how wonderful it was that I could go there any time I wanted, up into the sky."

And I am reminded that she is a child still.

We all are, really, Ethra, Cass and I. But Ethra more so.

"I need you to fly," I say. "Mydra has sent an outrider to Gafol. I need you to get there before him. Find my father. His is the roundhouse on the outer edge of the town, just before the barren land rolls into the Freewood. Find him. Take him to my Aunty Elsam. I will meet you there. And I need you to go now, even though it's dark."

"I'm not scared," she says.

"Give my father this," I say, handing her the broken sword. "So he will know you speak true. Tell him I am well. You will have to be quick. The grefa stones will start whistling the moment you arrive."

I hug her then and kiss her cheek.

"I will see you in a few days. A week at most."

"Any longer, and I will come looking for you."

Cass and I follow Ethra down the stairs and out of the tower. Cass hugs her, and I hug her again.

"Good luck, Ethra Kell-Clainh," I say.

"Luck is a bucket with a hole, Alys Clainh-Kell," she replies.

And then she is gone, up into the dark sky.

"I will wait until light before heading out," says Cass. There is a dressing across his nose and his eyes are black. "I am not as brave as Ethra."

It is chilly outside, and we go back into the Library.

"You are limping," says Cass as we near the top of the stairs. "Let me redress that wound."

"I can do it," I say.

"I can do it better," he replies.

I lie on the bed, positioning the blanket so only the wound is visible. He makes a salve of leaves and petals from Madec's chest and applies them gently.

"Why did you come back?" I ask.

"I was on the road to Leax, and I looked back over my shoulder and saw the statue at the gates. The statue of you. You looked fierce. And then I looked at the wolf, your companion. And I thought how fine it would be to have a wolf for a companion. A person with a wolf for a companion would be safe." He begins to apply the dressing over the salve, and his fingers briefly brush my thigh. "And then I realised you don't have a wolf for a companion. You have Ethra. And you have me." He covers my thigh with the blanket. "And I felt ashamed. And, also, I felt afraid for you."

"Thank you," I say. "For coming back."

I lean forward and kiss his cheek.

He smiles and kisses mine.

"You have old scars," he says. "Like me." He points to my scalp.

I nod, tracing a finger along the fine scar that runs from my hairline to the nape of my neck, the scar that was once the first of the Seven Cuts. And I do not hear the passage of the whetted flint. I hardly think about the Ritual at all.

"It's nothing," I say. "An ugly thing, but that is all."

"It is only a little scar," he says. "And you are prettier for it."

"We should get some sleep," I say, suddenly embarrassed. "We need to be up early."

"Of course," he says, rising.

I watch him as he makes a bed on the floor next to me.

"Will you help us?" I ask. "When you have freed your father?"

He crawls under his blanket.

"Yes," he says. "I will try my best to be your finewolf, Dracafysian. At least until your actual finewolf companion turns up."

"Don't call me that," I say, lying back. "Dracafysian. It seems silly."

"It does seem a little silly," he says, weariness creeping into his voice. "And also a little frightening."

In less than a minute, Casmel Durn is asleep and snoring.

It is an hour or more before sleep finds me. All I can think of is the Gravene, a monstrous being that has slaughtered who knows how many gods and laid waste to who knows how many heavens. And I, Alys Clainh, daughter and son of Aryc and Alva Clainh, am supposed to defeat it?

The very notion should have me trembling with fear. And yet it doesn't. And when sleep finally comes, it is a deep and peaceful thing.

Printed in Great Britain
by Amazon